*Scott Ballentine*

# Christ for Life

A Story of End Times

## Scott Ballentyne

Copyright © 2015 Scott Ballentyne.

All rights reserved. No part of this book may be used or reproduced by any means, graphic, electronic, or mechanical, including photocopying, recording, taping or by any information storage retrieval system without the written permission of the author except in the case of brief quotations embodied in critical articles and reviews.

WestBow Press books may be ordered through booksellers or by contacting:

WestBow Press
A Division of Thomas Nelson & Zondervan
1663 Liberty Drive
Bloomington, IN 47403
www.westbowpress.com
1 (866) 928-1240

Because of the dynamic nature of the Internet, any web addresses or links contained in this book may have changed since publication and may no longer be valid. The views expressed in this work are solely those of the author and do not necessarily reflect the views of the publisher, and the publisher hereby disclaims any responsibility for them.

Any people depicted in stock imagery provided by Thinkstock are models, and such images are being used for illustrative purposes only. Certain stock imagery © Thinkstock.

ISBN: 978-1-5127-1991-8 (sc)
ISBN: 978-1-5127-1993-2 (hc)
ISBN: 978-1-5127-1992-5 (e)

Library of Congress Control Number: 2015918881

Print information available on the last page.

WestBow Press rev. date: 1/29/2016

# Sources of information / Copyright permissions

Thank you to: www.kerusso.com for allowing me to use the Christ for Life logo and full cross picture. I strongly recommend wearing your faith! I have had many people comment on my Kerusso shirts when I wear them, as they spark conversation, and isn't that the point?!

Thank you to: Biblica Inc.
Scripture taken from Holy Bible, New International Version®, NIV®
Copyright © 1973, 1978, 1984, 2011, by Biblica, Inc®
Used by permission. All rights reserved worldwide.

Thank you to Hodder & Stoughton Ltd.
Scripture quotations [marked NIV] taken from the Holy Bible,
New International Version Anglicised
Copyright© 1979, 1984, 2011 Biblica,
Used by permission of Hodder &Stoughton
Ltd, an Hachette UK company
All rights reserved.
'NIV' is a registered trademark of Biblica
UK trademark number 1448790

Thank you to Zodervan.
"Scripture taken from the Holy Bible, New International Version®, NIV® Copyright© 1973, 1978, 1984, 2011 by Biblica, Inc.™
Used by permission of Zondervan. All rights reserved worldwide. WWW.ZONDERVAN.COM"

"The "NIV" and "New International Version" are trademarks registered in the United States Patent and Trademark Offices by Biblica, Inc.™"

Thank you to: Greg Durocher
USGS Office of Communications & Publishing
Science Information Services - Anchorage, Alaska
General Science & Alaska Questions: askusgs@usgs.gov
For providing a clearer picture to half truths and misinformation in the:
Oil Reserve E-mail I Received August 25, 2009

Thank you to: Scott McLeod, J.D., Ph.D.
Director of Innovation, Prairie Lakes AEA 8
www.dangerouslyirrelevant.org/contact
www.dangerouslyirrelevant.org/calendar

and thank you to: Karl Fisch karlfisch@gmail.com
For their work and permission to quote their, Did You Know video:
http://www.youtube.com/watch?v=cL9Wu2kWwSY&hd=1

Thank you to: Global Pulse for their permission to use quotes from their story: Food Price Crisis
Source: http://www.linktv.org/video/2527/food-price-crisis

**Food Price Crisis**
(Global Pulse: May 2, 2008) Global food prices soar and the world's poorest people go even hungrier. Food riots fuel political crises in some nations. Rich nations pledge more aid. Will it be enough to stop what some world leaders call "a silent tsunami of hunger"?
SOURCES: ABC News & NBC News, U.S.; BBC, U.K.; Al Jazeera English, Qatar; CCTV, China; 5 Day News, U.S.

Thank you to: bbc.co.uk/moreorless for their story Muslim Demographics – The Truth http://www.youtube.com/watch?v=mINChFxRXQs&hd=1 with 160,666 views (which was in response to Muslims demographics: You Tube video with over 14,762,726 million hits. 7.31 minutes http://www.youtube.com/watch?v=6-3X5hIFXYU) Once again a video exposed for having half truths and uncorroborated information. If you will take notice, the original video has almost 92 times more views. As my wife said "You cannot un-ring a bell."

Thank you to: The StarPhoenix, Heather Persson for confirming and allowing the use of the China Stockpiles Oil email I received. (Story dated June 30th, 2009 Regina Leader-Post by Joanne Peterson). Also Patricia Mohr Scotiabank's commodities expert. (Email confirmation of original story May 2014).

Thank you to: Wikipedia for enlightening me further on mis quotes and quotes out of context concerning a Charles Darwin quote.
http://en.wikipedia.org/wiki/Fallacy_of_quoting_out_of_context

The quote in context is: To suppose that the eye with all its inimitable contrivances for adjusting the focus to different distances, for admitting different amounts of light, and for the correction of spherical and chromatic aberration, could have been formed by natural selection, seems, I freely confess, absurd in the highest degree. Yet reason tells me, that if numerous gradations from a perfect and complex eye to one very imperfect and simple, each grade being useful to its possessor, can be shown to exist; if further, the eye does vary ever so slightly, and the variations be inherited, which is certainly the case; and if any variation or modification in the organ be ever useful to an animal under changing conditions of life, then the difficulty of believing that a perfect and complex eye could be formed by natural selection, though insuperable by our imagination, can hardly be considered real.

—Charles Darwin, *Origin of Species*

# PREFACE

If you are not a believer in Jesus Christ or God, I challenge you to read this book; after all, you are the one for whom I truly wrote this book. I wrote *Christ for Life* to provide an argument that the end of days could easily happen in our lifetime. Not that it necessarily will, but that it could, so why not be prepared? I originally added four chapters to the beginning of the book to lay the groundwork for an unbeliever or skeptic to believe in the possibility of Revelation. That writing consists of a lot of personal thoughts, YouTube video data, and random e-mails wrapped together to provide that platform, and it can be found in the afterword, at the end of the book. Feel free to read the afterword first if that kind of stuff interests you. This book is dedicated to you on your journey closer to God.

The title *Christ for Life* comes from every ounce of my being believing that we are created by God. All of creation cries out, "There is a God!" He is found in the complexity of the human body; he is found in the trees; he is found in fifty shades of green in the colors of the leaves; he is found in Christ. Darwin himself is quoted as saying, "To suppose that the (human) eye could have been formed by natural selection, seems, I freely confess, absurd in the highest degree."

I quoted this quote out of context because I think it's still relevant that Charles Darwin said it. People often quote the bible out of context as well to make it say what they want it to say. All that I'd ask is that you remember that the theory of evolution is just that—a theory, not a fact. (The quote in context can be found on the previous page in the Source of Information.)

I have purposely wrapped my story around the entire book of Revelation to not take anything away from what the Bible says. Please be wise and read Revelation yourself so you will not be easily fooled as to which is which.

I have two thoughts to share with you as you read this book. The first thought I'd like you to contemplate is this; Imagine the world as it is today with all the buildings, monuments, bridges and great manmade structures over the earth. Millions upon millions of things like cell phones, computers, houses, dishes, clothing, art work, and the list goes on and on. Now imagine every human is removed from the earth and all that is left is all the manmade stuff as well as all the animals, sea creatures, trees, mountains and everything that was not made by man but was here since the beginning of time as we know it. I think it would be impossible to deny that intelligent design had made all these manmade things on the earth. It would be impossible to fathom that they could have just appeared here from a single cell reproducing and mutating over and over again creating a single skyscraper made out of steel, glass and concrete, never mind all the detailed individualized possessions inside them as well as the stairs and elevators. No person could deny intelligent design in this case. Never mind the millions of buildings and structures the world over. Now take away every single manmade thing on the planet and focus on only the details of the planet itself. The mountains, the sea, volcanoes, rain, snow, sunshine, the animals, the sea creatures, they all scream out intelligent design. They all scream out "There is a God!" Look at your fingers and your toes, your eyes, feel your heart beating, feel your breath against your hand, look at all your veins and imagine all that blood being pumped all around your body by your heart to keep you alive. Now go try and build a life sized replica of a human baby with Lego and see if in a million years it will ever come to life and become a walking, talking, human being. I think any person would agree that it would be impossible. The complexity of the human brain, eyes, nervous, muscle, and blood system each alone are enough to say that they could only have been intelligently designed, never mind that they all work together and create movement, breath and life for each human, animal, and sea creature. That's not even including or considering all the individual cells that make up each of these things. For me it is undeniable that intelligent design exists. You can debate all you want about what religion is the one true way, or the truth, but the one thing you cannot deny is the existence of intelligent design in the creation of life, the earth, and the universe as a whole.

The second thought I'd like you to ponder is an analogy of a pilot flying a plane as it's compared to a person trying to get to heaven. The pilot is on a very long flight and is paying little or no attention to his navigational equipment or to his environment. Every few minutes the plane is one more degree off course. At the end of the ten hour flight the pilot is nowhere near his planned destination but instead has found himself totally turned around and going in the opposite direction. The pilot finally figures out that the plane is in the middle of nowhere surrounded by ocean, hundreds of miles from anywhere and completely out of fuel. Full of tears the pilot regrets his poor decisions that now have lead to his ultimate death. Now imagine a person on the narrow road to heaven. Month after month and year after year the Devil whispers in their ear trying to sway them away from God. The worlds many sins tempt the person as they walk side by side the other people in the world. Year after year the person never checks the instruments that God gave them to see if they are still on course for their planned destination of heaven and one day the person dies. A few moments later they find themselves in front of God being judged and they are shocked to find out they are not going to be allowed into heaven. The person starts to cry as God says to them, "When was the last time you talked to me; read my word, or pursued me in anyway? You are way off course and have found yourself now in the total opposite direction. Your name has not been written in the book of life. I have made no place for you here."

## Chapter 1

# Falling (A look ahead)

Monday, July 31, 2051

The global population is in steady decline after a series of catastrophic events, including the recent attacks on Canada and Mexico. It is estimated that in the last three months, billions of people around the world have died from wars, starvation, or religious persecution. Today when I turned on the television, all I could see was death and destruction on every channel. The Arab nations of Pakistan, Iran, and Iraq were being blamed for releasing some sort of chemical weapon over Israel that was believed to have killed well over a hundred thousand Jews who lived there. One man dared to give an exact number. He said, "The number is one hundred and forty-four thousand, and with that the fate of the world is sealed."

I thought to myself, *That number sounds familiar,* and at just that moment, all the power went out in my house—well, if you could still call it a house. It was barely standing after the recent earthquake. I was sure that as soon as the structural engineers came next week, they would deem it unsafe and book it for demolishing. Then what?

I gave my head a shake to get back into reality. It was light outside, so I could see the front street clearly since the blinds were open. It was quite odd, I thought—the message of the 144,000, I mean, not the light. I looked at my watch. It was 7:00 a.m. I went to the fridge and pulled out the milk. I sat down, poured myself a bowl of cereal, and contemplated shooting myself right there at the kitchen table. My gun was within reach, so it would hardly take any effort. I wouldn't even have to get up.

I thought to myself, *Why did we go visit my friend Janice in Wawanesa the first weekend of April? Why did the van break down so that we had to stay there for a week waiting for parts? I wish I had been in Winnipeg and that the nuclear bomb had landed square on my head. At least I wouldn't be here still trying to pick up the pieces months later, only to be followed by an earthquake. Really, an earthquake? We live in, excuse my French, Winnipeg, not in San Francisco. We're not supposed to have earthquakes here!* Just then my nine-year-old son, Stephan, came up from behind me and said, "Love you, Declan. What's for breakfast?"

"Cereal," I said as I pulled the gun toward me. "Go wake up the clan for me, will you?" It was more of a telling than an asking, and he knew it.

With that, he yelled at the top of his lungs, "Get up, you lazy buggers." I looked at him and rolled my eyes. He shrugged and said, "What? Did you want me to go wake eighty people up one by one like Mom would do?"

Stephan had become my son by marriage but also by choice, just like his sisters, Amelia and Amanda, who were now seventeen and sixteen. My biological son, Colin, had gone back home to his mother's yesterday, like he did every Sunday night for the week until I picked him up on Friday again.

"No," I said. How could I blame him? I was about to wake them up with a gunshot. His way was definitely a lot less messy. Eighty people, I can't believe eighty people even fit in my house, never mind that I would "let" them in. Since the food shortage, though, what was I supposed to do, let my friends and neighbors starve to death? Ask me now and I'd say yes! Let them all starve, they drive me crazy!

"Oh," I said. "Love you too, Stephan."

As the "clan" filtered in, I zoned out and turned on my mp3 radio as I walked out the front door. The reception seemed very fuzzy. I checked the time: 7:32 a.m. A girl giving the daily news said, "There seems to be a province-wide power outage, and the only reason we're able to broadcast is because of the backup generators we have. It also seems like the power outage might be more widespread and that for now, all flights are canceled to and from anywhere in the country."

I thought to myself, *Not like I care. I haven't been anywhere since 2010, when I went on a mission trip with my church.*

She went on to say, "The Manitoba government tells us that we should expect it to be months before uninterrupted power can be expected, considering the damage from the earthquake and all the rubble that has to be cleaned up before workers can access all the downed power lines and blown transformers."

I got to work a couple of hours later. You never realize how far away somewhere is until you have to walk there. My boss, Jeff, was already there with both overhead doors opened up. "The power is out, and I couldn't see inside unless I opened the doors," he told me.

I just nodded and walked inside. We talked for a bit like we always did, and I asked him if I could use the work van for personal use because mine had been written off after a tree fell on it during the earthquake. I knew it wouldn't be a problem, but I still asked. When I went to leave the shop to start my day, the van wouldn't start. I tried ten times to get it to start, but it wouldn't turn over. "Eish. Stupid alternator," I muttered. The alternator had been going for the past two months. I carried a new one with me in the van because we knew it was going to fail eventually. I got out and removed the new alternator from the box and proceeded to get some of the tools I needed. My boss popped the hood for me and guided me through the process of removing the old alternator. Two hours later, we finally had the alternator in—*we* meaning me. I cleaned up a little as Jeff got in the driver's seat and tried to start the van. Still the van wouldn't start.

"Did you do it right?" he asked.

"Yes, I did. I did exactly what you said!" I answered back.

"Are you out of gas again, Declan?" Jeff jabbed.

"No. That was one time. Give me a break. I filled up yesterday after work!" I bellowed back. "Beautiful day. I guess we'll have to get it towed." I picked up the phone, but it was dead. I put it back, opened my cell phone, dialed the number, and hit "send," but nothing happened. It just kept searching for a signal. "Jeff, try your cell. I can't get a signal." I walked outside to see if I could get a better signal. I noticed out on the front street that there were no cars going by, even though it was normally quite busy. Instead there were a few vehicles parked with the doors wide open and their occupants outside trying to use their cell phones with no luck either, it seemed. "Do you have a signal, Jeff?" I asked.

"No" was his only reply.

I walked to the front street and looked down in both directions. Nothing was moving. As far as I could see, there were just dead cars with people standing around trying to use their cell phones. I heard a dull noise getting louder. At first I couldn't make it out, but then it became clearer and closer. It was screaming. In the distance, from the south, I could see people running and screaming, but seconds after they started running, I saw them falling. As their lifeless bodies dropped to the ground, a man behind me screamed, "Cover your mouth. It's probably an airborne chemical!" and with that he too fell to the ground. My head started to feel light. I tried to run, but I could feel myself falling, and my eyes slowly closed. The last thing I saw was my watch flashing in front of my face: 1:00 p.m. July 31, 1:00 p.m. July 31, 1:00 p.m. July 31.

*Wake up, wake up, wake up,* I kept telling myself. *Wake up!* Slowly I opened my eyes. All I could see were white lines. I rubbed my eyes and finally notice how uncomfortable I was. I stretched and creaked as my neck and back cracked back into place. I opened my eyes once again to see the white lines in front of my face. I lifted my head a little and saw the asphalt, and then it dawned on me where I was. I was still on the road. I stood up and looked around; the cars were still all around, and cell phones lay here and there on the ground. There were still lots of people lying on the ground, and only about half of them were moving around.

I looked at my watch, which was now flashing 3:00 p.m. It seemed as though whatever had happened, I had been out for a couple of hours and so had everyone else. I was groggy, but I walked back over to the shop and called out for Jeff. "Jeff? Jeff? Where are you?" I checked under and in the van we had been working on and didn't find him. Still I called out his name. "Jeff, it isn't funny anymore!" Not like it was funny at the beginning. I walked upstairs, but he wasn't up there either. I went back down and looked around some more. Both the work vans were still there, and so was Jeff's Hummer. I pulled out my cell phone and called his number, and it started to ring. I took the phone away from my ear and could hear his phone ringing somewhere in the shop. Finally I pinpointed it. It seemed to be coming from the bathroom. I called out to him, but again he never answered. I closed my cell phone and the ringing stopped. I unlocked the bathroom and saw Jeff lying on the floor.

"Wake up, Jeff, wake up." He didn't move. "Jeff! Wake up! Come on, man, you have to get up!" I knelt down, and I couldn't hear him breathing. Jeff had a condition called sleep apnea, which meant that while he slept he would sometimes stop breathing. Normally he had a machine that helped force more air into his system so his oxygen levels didn't go so low that he stopped breathing. I leaned in really close, listening with my left ear since I'm practically deaf in my right. Closer still I leaned in up to his mouth, but I couldn't hear or feel a thing. I touched his face with my hand. It was cold. I opened his eyes, but I could see that he was already gone. I pulled at his legs to straighten his body out and noticed it didn't want to straighten out like a limp body would normally. Not that I pulled a lot of dead bodies around, but I had dragged the kids around from time to time as we played. His body seemed stiff. I knelt down again and tried to do CPR for a few minutes. I knew it was hopeless, but part of me wanted to believe he wasn't dead. The logical side of me knew he had been dead for a couple of hours and that nobody could have saved him. Nobody could have saved any of them.

Just then my cell phone rang. ICE is the name that came up, 867-5309. *ICE* stands for "in case of emergency," a.k.a. my home phone number. I had read in an e-mail a few years back that having such a number in your cell phone would be helpful to police and paramedics if you were unable to provide the information to them. They could just look on your phone and not wonder who they should call first. "Hello," I said as I answered it, expecting it to be my wife, Marie.

"Hello," she said. "Your wife is dead." Then I realized it wasn't Marie. It was her sister Lori. Her sister was never one to mince words and just told it how it was, but this was over the top.

"What do you mean?" I asked as I felt the tears well up in my eyes. The shock made me sit down.

"I mean she's dead, stiff, not moving, not breathing, cold and all that—dead. So are your mom and Stephan, Ethan, and my mom and dad too. Along with everyone else who was at home when it happened." Then she said, "Check your watch, check your phone. What time does it say?"

I could already tell it was a loaded question, but I looked anyway. "3:10 p.m. Why?"

"And what time was it before you were knocked out?" she asked.

How did she know that had happened to me? With that, the bottom fell out from my stomach, and I felt tears roll down my cheeks. I choked on my emotions as I said, "One."

For the first time ever in the five years I had known Lori, I could hear her crying on the phone. "It happened here at 1:00 p.m., too. You have to come home, Declan."

Since the food shortage, Lori and her boyfriend, Ethan, my mother-in-law and father-in-law, as well as seventy other people had been living at our house because nobody could make ends meet on their own. It cost your left leg just to feed yourself, never mind to pay for rent or a mortgage. "You have to come home, Declan. I haven't heard from the girls either." The girls (Amelia and Amanda) would have been at school when it happened.

"Okay, I know. I'll be right there in fifteen minutes," I said. I hung up my phone, went over to my work van, inserted the key into the ignition, and turned the key. Just like I expected, it started. I turned it back off and got out of the van. I had an eerie feeling that the van not starting and all the stalled vehicles outside was God performing "controlled chaos." Before I closed the door to the shop and locked it, I yelled out one more time, "Jeff!" I wished so much that he would respond, but I knew he wouldn't answer, and he didn't. I grabbed the keys to his Hummer and locked the shop door. I wasn't going to take the van when I could take the Hummer, that's for sure.

It was a little more difficult than you might think, driving home, because there were still quite a few vehicles abandoned all over the road. It was like swerving around cones on an obstacle course but these were cars and trucks, not little cones that you could run over. In some places vehicles were side by side, making it impossible to get around them. The most disturbing part was seeing dead bodies lying all over the place with flies starting to swarm around some of them. I saw a couple of crows on the chest of a dead woman near a crosswalk. They were proceeding to do nature's work. It made me literally want to vomit, so I rolled down the window just in case.

Eventually I had to take the side streets all the way home because the main street was too blocked with dead bodies and vehicles. There were more people on the road now, like me, taking the side streets to wherever they were going. You could see it in their eyes that they were lost and confused. It felt like 9/11 again. The disbelief in their eyes and the look on their faces said, "I need to get home and see if this is real." I finally got home a half hour later, and that's when I knew it really was real. I could "feel" they were all gone as I stepped out of the truck. Oh, how alone I felt. Even though Lori was there, I still felt utterly and hopelessly alone. Although I hadn't confirmed it yet, I knew my ten-year-old son Colin was gone too, and I started to cry again.

I walked up to the house, where Lori was on the front step. She had my Bible opened to a page toward the end of the book. She asked me, "What do you think happened?"

Lori was a lot of things, but two things she was not were naive or dumb. She knew what had happened. Otherwise my Bible would not be at page 3160, Revelation 7. It was a parallel Bible I had borrowed from a good man and a good pastor named Patrick Clark. I had borrowed it a long time ago. Anyway, I was sure he was dead now, so I wouldn't have to worry about returning it. I said to her, "Lori, I'd wager that there are about 2.5 billion people who are dead right now, and another 2.5 billion wishing it was them instead."

# Chapter 2

# Taken (A look ahead)

What an awful feeling, to be left behind. I can't remember one happy thought that ever came from feeling left behind. We've all had our disappointments, but think back to the time when your dad first left you and your mom. How much it hurt when he said, "We just can't make it work." How much it hurt every day when you prayed and wished for him to come back and he never did. Occasionally he would tell you that he wanted to move back to town, and you believed him. It wasn't until you were in your twenties that you finally admitted that it was all a lie. When he left you at two years old, he never looked back, and he was never coming back. That's how abandoned I felt right now again. This time it wasn't my father not coming back; now it was my wife, two sons, two daughters, my mom, and my mother- and father-in-law—and that's just the people I know of right now who are dead. They have all been taken.

I got up from the step after about ten minutes of talking to Lori about everything we had both experienced in the last hour. I slowly searched the house room by room, finding my family amongst the other dead guests in my house. I didn't want to find what I knew I would find, so I was in no hurry to find them. In the living room I found my mother- and father-in-law as well as my mom. I didn't have to look long before I found my wife, Marie. She was in the kitchen facedown on the table with a cup of coffee close by. I didn't bother to lift her head; I didn't want to see the face of death again. Seeing Jeff dead and all those people dead on the street was enough for me. I chose to remember my wife the way she was as I kissed her lips and went off to work each morning.

It wasn't until I went upstairs that I found Stephan sitting cross-legged in Colin's room. I wondered why he was here; he should have been at school. It seems he was playing with YuGioh cards before he was taken. I knelt down and kissed the top of his head and gave him one last hug. As I stood up, I could feel a tear start to well up in my right eye and then one in my left, and then they wouldn't stop. I sat down beside him and wept like I did as a boy. If I thought I had a reason to cry as a child, oh, how much more I cried now.

After a few minutes, I forced myself up and entered my bedroom. It used to be for just Marie and me, but now it held the remains of one of the other four couples who shared our room. *Well, that's two fewer people to share a room with,* I thought to myself. The other three couples would have already been at work when the rapture happened, so at least I wouldn't have to figure out what to do with their bodies. All I knew was that I had a total of sixteen dead bodies that I had to deal with. *Where are Sugar and Sydney anyway?* I wondered. I slowly made my way downstairs to the basement to find another couple of bodies. My dog Sugar was licking one of the bodies, and my cat Sydney was doing the same. The bodies were two of our neighbors who lost their house to foreclosure because they couldn't afford the inflated price of food and still afford their home. I picked up the cat and walked upstairs and called for Sugar to "come." She wagged her stubby little border collie tail and ran up after me. I walked outside and sat on the front step and began petting the cat and the dog.

I'd always known about the rapture. I just always assumed I'd be taken; maybe that was my downfall. I had been so consumed by the story of Revelation and the awesome visual imagery that I got from it, that I had focused more on the story than on making sure I'd be ready for it. The rapture was what was supposed to happen after the 144,000 Jews were sealed. Many believed that the rapture would happen after twelve thousand Jews from each of the original twelve tribes were martyred or murdered.

I asked Lori to help me remove the dead bodies from the house starting with my mother- and father-in-law from the front living room, she nodded her head yes reluctantly. I put the cat down beside me on the step and got up and stretched a little. It wasn't going to be easy to get all those bodies out of the house. We started with my father-in-law, Peter. Lori grabbed her dad's feet and I grabbed his upper body under the arms like a fireman would do, and we dragged him out the front door.

Now the question was what to do with all the bodies. What were other people going to do with the bodies that they had in their houses? Lori and I brought Peter's body out to the front curb and proceeded to go get my mother-in-law Cindy's body. For now we would bring all the bodies to the curb and then figure out what to do with them. I had to place a sheet over Marie's body before we carried her out. I just couldn't bear to look at her. I felt as though I had let her down by not being with her. Although it was impossible, I imagined she was crying, looking down on me from heaven. We propped her up against the maple tree outside by the curb, and then I went to go get Stephan myself. As I passed the closet, I grabbed a few more sheets to cover all the bodies. I wrapped them all as best I could to help prevent stray animals or the flies from getting to them until I knew what to do.

By the time we got the now eighteen bodies out of the house, and all wrapped up, we were both exhausted. As I sat down again on the front step, I noticed a cop car down the street a bit, so I tried to flag him over. At first the officer just flashed his lights at me. After a couple of minutes, he finally pulled up and shut off the car, but he didn't bother to get out of his vehicle. It was hard to miss the pile of dead bodies, and I could tell he was deeply disturbed by the sight of them. He said, "One of your neighbours called and said they thought they had Charles Manson living down the street from them."

"Why's that?" I asked rhetorically.

He gestured with his hands spread to the bodies that lay to the left and to the right of him and asked, "What's this about?"

I replied, "The rapture happened. I had eighteen dead bodies in my house that were going to start smelling and decaying. I didn't know what else to do with them."

He scoffed and mocked me, repeating, "The rapture, hey? Turn on the radio and they'll tell you what to do with the bodies and what you should do over the next couple of days." Then he turned back on his car and slowly started to drive off.

I yelled out, "What station?"

*Christ for Life*

He stopped the vehicle, poked his head out the window looking back, and said in a dull voice, "All of them."

After listening to the radio for a while, we walked back to the front street. *We don't have time to wait around for a "death truck" to come pick up the bodies,* I thought to myself. I contemplated: now what were we supposed to do, and where were we supposed to go? I didn't know. All I knew was that I didn't want to be here when the scavengers came out. If history had taught me anything, it was that there will always be people who loot, steal, and kill for profit when a disaster happens. Just look at what happened when Hurricane Katrina hit New Orleans. I thought we better get started then and be one step ahead of them. I said to Lori, "Lori, go break in next door and get whatever food doesn't have to be refrigerated, and look for jewelry and money."

"Why?" is all she asked.

"Because we have no cash, and if we don't do it now, someone else will, and we will starve to death. Until the bullets start flying, I don't think anybody's going to listen now, considering all that's happened." That was good enough for her. She headed over to the house across the street and reached her hand through the already busted front door window to unlock the door. After she went inside, I went to my backyard and opened the door to my garage, which was still for the most part standing strong after the previous month's earthquake. I retrieved a box of firewood I had and a jerry can of gas I used for the lawn mower and snow blower through the years. I brought them out to the front street and stacked the whole box of firewood over my family's dead bodies. Then I poured most of the twenty litres of gasoline over the wood and the sheets covering the bodies. After that was done, I made a trail of gasoline to the other side of the street.

"Our father, who art in heaven, hallowed be thy name. Thy kingdom come, thy will be done, on earth as it is in heaven. Give us this day our daily bread; and forgive us our trespasses as we forgive those who trespass against us. And lead us not into temptation, but deliver us from evil. For thine is the kingdom, and the power, and the glory, forever and ever. Amen." After a long pause I lit the gasoline. As it raced toward the other side of the street, I said, "Please forgive me." At that moment, I heard a mighty *swoosh* as the fumes ignited and a tremendous ball of flames shot up from the pile.

I turned to Jeff's Hummer and unlocked the door. Lori came out with bags full of food and a baseball bat under one arm. She looked at the burning bodies, and then looked at me. She stopped for a second but then went to the truck, put the stuff in, and went to the next house. I went to my side of the street, and we continued to collect things from the houses we could until the truck was almost full. We drove to the end of our block and turned up Arlington, stopping at the Tesco station for gas. The pump wouldn't turn on, so I went inside, and that's when I noticed that the attendant was already dead on the floor. Not from the rapture—it seemed he had died from two shots in the chest. The killings had already started. I got behind the counter and hit the proper buttons to turn the pump on. Then I grabbed four jerry cans off the shelf and went outside to fill up the truck with gas and the jerry cans with diesel. I asked Lori to go in and get us something to eat and asked her to grab the microwave when she was finished. She came back out with a gun and some bullets she had found in the office as well as the bank deposit that the previous person had missed after shooting the attendant. I guess the other person was in too much of a hurry. Within five minutes we were back on the road and I was headed back to the shop where I worked. I guess now, it was use to work, because there was no way I was hanging around here!

Although I was 99 percent certain that my son Colin had been taken, I was still drawn to go to his mom's house, just to check. When we arrived, there were others in the parking lot outside their town house, eyeing us up. I told Lori to guard the truck while I checked inside. The windows were all busted out from the earthquake, but I couldn't reach in through the window on the door without cutting my arm so I kicked the door open. Someone half yelled, "What are you doing?" but all I did was look at them before walking in to search the house.

There were a few people dead here and there, but I didn't know any of them, so I carried on with my search. I honestly didn't expect to find Colin here anyway, so after I was finished, we drove over to my son's school, which was basically a stone's throw away from their house. I wasn't going to find him alive there either, it seemed. I saw thirty or forty adults already outside, crying and hugging each other, but there didn't seem to be any children anywhere.

I assumed these people were parents just like me, but I didn't have time to stand around and cry right now. I quickly ran into the school and found my son's lifeless body bent over his desk. I had to yank on his body to get him loose of his desk, and then I carried him out to the vehicle. I had to put his body on top of the Hummer and strap it down, because there was no more room in the truck. I knew that the other parents were staring at me in disbelief, but I didn't have time to explain myself to these people. Now was the time to get out of Dodge, as the saying goes. As we drove to the shop, I got Lori to keep phoning Amanda and Amelia just in case they were still alive, but she got no response. We didn't have time to keep looking for people who were most likely dead. All that would do is put our own lives in danger, considering the chaos that I knew was coming.

Man, if I thought it took a long time getting home, it seemed to take twice as long to get back to work from the school. Everywhere we looked there was destruction and dead bodies. I just wanted to get back to the shop and switch everything into our newest work van, a two-year-old diesel Sprinter. Apparently they were great on fuel. We hadn't even insured the van yet, but I guess we were going to put it to the test. It had a bunch of shelving in it, so it would be great for sorting everything later so we could easily find everything. Just as we turned onto Main Street from Leila, *Smash!* "What the?" I shouted. Somebody had just rear-ended us, very hard. I started to slow down to see what was going on and it happened again. *SMASH!*

Lori screamed, "He's trying to run us off the road!"

My only thought was that he wanted our truck full of supplies, and with that thought, I swerved hard to the left and got in the other lane. I slammed on the brakes and yelled, *"Do something!"*

Without hesitation, Lori lifted the gun from under her leg. The man's vehicle came up quickly beside us, and she aimed squarely at her target and put a bullet in him. His car was still moving forward, but after hitting a parked car and then a tree, it finally came to a stop. The man still had his foot on the gas even though it was obvious he was dead. I put the truck in park, quickly rushed to his driver's-side door, pulled him out of the car, and turned it off. I looked down at the man, and for good measure, I wanted to kick him as hard as I could with my steel-toed boots but I restrained myself. Man, did he tick me off though! I looked in the backseat and found a full backpack, so I grabbed it. I took the keys out of the ignition and went back and opened the trunk. There was a large hockey bag and I tried to pull it out, but it was quite heavy and then it started to move! I dropped the backpack in surprise but then opened the zipper of the hockey bag. It moved again. I stepped back a bit. I'm telling you, I was freaked out! The bag continued to move and eventually opened more to expose a half-naked woman gagged and tied up. I'm not going to lie: she wasn't ugly. I didn't have a knife, so I opened the backpack and dumped it out onto the ground. Sure enough, I found a knife amongst the articles that a sick and twisted man would have to rape and torture his victim.

At this time Lori started coming out of the truck to see what was going on. I told the woman, "I'm not going to hurt you" as I put up my hands to symbolize my intentions. "I'm just going to cut the ropes off your wrists and then give the knife to you, okay?" She nodded yes, so I cut the ropes off the lady's wrists and handed her the knife. By now Lori was at the back of the car and looking at the contents of the backpack on the ground. She also saw the practically naked woman getting out of the trunk.

I gave the woman my jacket and escorted her to the truck, passing on the other side of the vehicle so she didn't have to see what her fate would have been if this guy had had his way with her. Lori came and opened the back hatch of the Hummer and gave the lady a blanket, a pair of her jeans, and a sweater. The clothes were obviously too big, but she graciously accepted them saying, "Thank you. My name is Michelle." We all exchanged names, and Lori grabbed a jerry can and went back and slowly poured some of the fuel onto the man's body and then the belongings of his backpack. She pulled out her lighter and lit the gasoline. She wished the man was still alive, for that was the punishment she felt he deserved.

As Lori came back to the truck, I realized we didn't have room for three people. I asked Michelle, "Do you want to come with us? Do you want us to leave you here, or do you want to be dropped off on the way out of town?"

"Where you going?" is all she asked.

"We don't know yet, other than far and north," I replied.

"North it is, then," she responded.

I asked Lori for the gun and climbed onto the roof of the truck, because there really wasn't enough room for three and we were only six blocks away from my work. I made sure that I was hanging on and that I was watching for another attack. I wouldn't let that happen again. We got to my workplace and transferred all the stuff into the Sprinter. Luckily it was already full of fuel. There was another empty jerry can at the shop, so we grabbed that as well. I looked in our shop fridge and grabbed my three packs of Pepsi and Jeff's water from the top shelf. There were a couple of pieces of Babel cheese and a stick of pepperoni on the fridge door shelf, so I grabbed those as well.

I closed the fridge and brought that stuff to the Sprinter. As I put it on the shelving, I realized I had forgotten something in the fridge. I went back, opened the fridge door, slid open the crisper, and smiled when I saw twelve beautiful bottles of Coors Lite lying there. I grabbed one and cracked it open. I took a big swig and lifted my head with a sigh. I put the rest in a box and opened the freezer. Jackpot! There was a bottle of Crown Royal, three quarters full. I smiled again as I took it, because I remembered there were two other bottles on the steel shelf by the bathroom that were supposed to go to one of our customers as a Christmas present. Oh well, too bad for them. I grabbed the two of them and put them in the box as well.

I took another sip of my beer, walked over to the Sprinter, and offered the girls a drink. Michelle said no, but Lori grabbed the open bottle of Crown and took a swig bigger than that of any man I ever saw take! She too sighed, and then sat down in the driver's seat of the Sprinter. I walked back into the shop and looked on the shelf where I had my invoices, lifted them up, and took the six hundred dollars from the cash sales I had done from my Thompson run. I went to the bathroom and rolled Jeff over to find his wallet. I opened the wallet to find another five hundred bucks and a few credit cards. I didn't think those would be any good anymore, but I took them just in case. "Sorry Jeff," I whispered. I walked out of the bathroom, closed the door, and turned off the light. I locked up the shop and told Lori to take the Sprinter and drive up Highway 6 as far as we could possibly get away from anyone. I would drive the Hummer for now as protection.

Michelle asked if she could come with me, but Lori quickly said, "He just lost his wife and all his family. I think he needs some time to himself." She was right.

# Chapter 3

# The Beginning of the End (A look back)

In 1979, Frank Newton of California introduced a prototype for the biochip transponder or, as it would be better known, an ID chip or microchip. By 1991, zoos around the world were micro chipping their animals. From there it carried through to pets and then to all animals that were destined for human consumption. Simply put, a small computer chip was injected just under the skin of the animal.

The chip had remained the size of a grain of rice, but since 2036, with the advancement of newer technology, it had had the memory storage capacity of a small computer. It had every piece of information that you could possibly ever want to know about the specimen in question. It started off simply with the specimen's complete family tree, date of insemination, birth date, sex, weight, height, and even an uploaded picture. Every shot, every checkup, everything deemed the least bit relevant was recorded on the chip. The chip also had global positioning capability and used it to track where the specimen went, but just as important, what other chipped specimens it came in contact with. Each time the specimen came within a set distance of another chipped specimen, the chips recorded the date, time, place, and duration of contact.

After mad cow, the bird flu, and other diseases played havoc with the markets, the G20 countries got smart and wanted to cut the overall losses to a minimum. Instead of killing off a whole herd of suspected infected cows, if one tested positive for a communicable disease, any animal it was in contact with was immediately destroyed. More tests would be done on the animals that were left, and if no other animals showed signs of being contaminated, they would be cleared for market. With this new chip, farmers and countries insulated themselves from huge losses and a greater amount of consumer trust in the meat industry was achieved. In recent years the chip had taken on the name Natas.

Armed with the knowledge that the chip was also being used in some human trials, some religious groups had been up in arms, believing the chip could represent the mark of Satan or the number of the beast. Still others looked forward to the day such advancements would help control the criminal element of the world's population, and didn't fear any religious ramifications.

After years of escalating violence, thefts and public protests, China had been the first to wage war on all criminal activity and pursued the use of the Natas chip in humans. First they followed Britain's lead and installed video surveillance on many of the streetlights and hydro poles in major cities. This became a huge strain on the prisons, but soon China got wise and ordered their peace officers to perform instant justice for all petty crimes and violations. Instead of going to jail, you got a very public flogging by the police. They also passed a law making it illegal to video- or audiotape any on-duty police officer, which prevented any police officer from being tried or even charged with assault. If you did videotape them, they would beat you to within an inch of your death and then made sure that they destroyed the evidence and the video camera. The public beatings were effective, but serious crimes were still on the rise, so in 2038, China was the first country to pass the New Advanced Technology Achieving Safety program or Natas for short. This new Natas program was initiated to create a greater sense of security within the population. All current inmates were ordered to have the Natas chip implanted in their right hand. The chip was designed exactly like the one that they put into animals except they added a tamperproof device. If the inmate tried to break or remove the chip, it sent a shock similar to a taser through the nervous system. If the chip was tampered with in any way, it would take them to their knees. They tested it on some of the toughest inmates around, and they were all literally crying for the pain to stop.

Only the Natas security team had the means to reset the chip's tamperproof device. It generally took them a couple of minutes to reset the chip after they were given the okay by the warden. You might try to tamper with the chip once, but you'd never be stupid enough to do it twice. The corrections officers knew they'd have a riot on their hands if they tried to inject all of the inmates with the chip at the same time. They also knew it made the most sense, so they petitioned the government to use a sleeping gas throughout the prisons and then inject the prisoners while they were out. The officers got their wish, and in the spring of 2038, every inmate in all of China was injected with the Natas chip. All incoming prisoners after that were to be administered the sleeping gas individually in a confined holding cell and then injected with the chip.

In a desperate and daring escape an inmate had actually cut off his own right hand to escape a medium-risk prison. The inmate was on the run for twenty days before a corner store clerk phoned in about a suspicious man with a blood-soaked sleeve tucked close to his body. The inmate's arm was so infected that the doctors had to amputate his whole right arm. When the man was finally returned to the prison, the guards were initially perplexed about where to inject him with a new Natas chip. After a short discussion, one of the guards is quoted as saying, "Let's put it in his forehead. He can't cut it out there!" After they all had a good laugh, that's exactly what they did. From that day forward, all inmates in China were administered the Natas chip in their foreheads instead of their hands. To further the reach of the Natas system, all freed inmates were restricted from entering any major city. It was a simple law to enforce, considering the GPS tracking that came with the Natas chip.

China quickly became the safest place on earth, and Westerners started coming to China to get away from all the hostilities of their homelands. Since they initiated the New Advanced Technology Achieving Safety program, people with wealth had been flooding to China like rats fleeing a sinking ship. China had always been a densely overpopulated place, and with all the new people migrating there in 2039, they passed a law that any new building had to have a minimum of twenty floors and at least half of it had to be for residential use. Single-family homes had been and continued to be expropriated and demolished on a daily basis to make way for the new world. It was a world made of steel and concrete, with skyscrapers everywhere. You could find more grass and trees in a museum than you'd find in all of Beijing. This all started in the early years of the century, but nobody cared because it wasn't happening in their backyard. The new buildings were supposed to help with the housing shortages, but in many places it had become the new homes of society's elite, selling on average for $500 million a floor. The mansions of Hollywood and Beverly Hills weren't where it was at any more since stalkers, obsessed fans, and paparazzi drove so many celebrities away. In China the actors and actresses are now revered like god's and at a god's command someone like a paparazzi or stalker will have their legs broken by a more than willing bodyguard. It was actually common for bodyguards to carry a taser in hand and a pistol holstered in their jacket. If you didn't listen the first time, you got tased. The second time, you got your legs broken. The next time you'd likely have a bullet in the back of your head. All seemed safe in China.

# Chapter 4

# To the Seven Churches

"Blessed is he who reads aloud the words of the prophecy. Those who listened to it being read and do what it says will also be blessed. For the time is near when these things will all come true." (Revelation 1:3) NIV (All bible quotes will be from the NIV bible except those in [    ])

John, who was one of Jesus' disciples, wrote to the seven churches that were in Asia [Turkey].

"See he's coming [arriving] with the clouds, and every eye will see him, everyone who pierced him; and all the nations [tribes] of the earth will weep in sorrow and in terror [wail] when he comes [because or on account of him].

"I'm the Alpha [the beginning] and the omega [ending], [of all things]" says the Lord God, who is and was and who is to come, the almighty.

It is I, your brother John, a fellow sufferer for the lord's sake, who am writing this letter to you. I too, have shared the patience Jesus gives, and we shall share his kingdom! I was on the island of Patmos, exiled there for preaching the word of God, and for telling what I knew about Jesus Christ. It was the Lord's day and I was worshiping, when suddenly I heard a loud voice behind me, a voice that sounded like the trumpet blast, saying, "I am the a and z, the first and last!" and then I heard him say, write down everything you see, and send a letter [book] to the seven churches in Asia [now Turkey]. (Revelation 1:7–11)

When I turned to see who was speaking, there behind me were seven candlesticks of gold. And standing among them was one who looked like Jesus who called himself the son of man, wearing a long robe circled with the golden band across his chest [golden girdle round his breast]. His hair was white as wool or snow, and his eyes penetrated like flames of fire. His feet gleamed like burnished bronze [fine brass glowing in a furnace], and his voice thundered like waves against the shore [sound of many waters]. He held seven stars in his right hand and a sharp, double bladed sword in his mouth, and his face shone like the power of the sun in the unclouded brilliance. When I saw him, I fell at his feet as dead; but he laid his right hand on me and said, "Don't be afraid! Though I am the first and last. The living one who died, who is now alive forever more, who has the keys of hell [hades] and death, don't be afraid! Write down what you've just seen, and what will soon be shown to you. This is the meaning of the seven stars you saw in my right hand, and the seven golden candlesticks: the seven stars are the leaders of the seven churches, and the seven candlesticks are the church's themselves." (Revelation 1:12–20)

Jesus tells John to write to the seven churches that he's coming. Jesus praises the churches for the good they are doing but is unafraid to tell them their shortcomings and what they must do better. He tells them to repent of their ways and to get back on the path of the righteousness (to follow God). Jesus seems to be especially angry with the church of Laodicea (seventh church), for he says to them, "I know you well, you are neither hot nor cold; I wish you were one or the other! But since you're merely lukewarm, I will spit you out of my mouth! You say, 'I'm rich, with everything I want; I don't need a thing!' And you don't realize that spiritually you are wretched and miserable and poor and blind and naked." (Revelation 3:15–17)

When Jesus talks to the seven churches, he could very well be talking about the seven different kinds of Christians that we can be.

> To the first he says, "I know how many good things you're doing. I know you don't tolerate sin amongst your members and you carefully examined the claims of those who say they are apostles but aren't. You found out how they lie. You have patiently suffered for me without quitting. Yet there's one thing wrong; you don't love me as at first!" (Revelation 2:2–4)

The love and drive for God can fade away unless you are constantly renewing and applying your love for him.

> To the second church Jesus says, "I know how much you suffer for the Lord, and I know all about your poverty [but you have heavenly riches!]. I know the slander of those opposing you, who say that they are Jews the children of God but they aren't, for they support the cause of Satan. Stop being afraid of what you are about to suffer for the Devil will soon throw some of you into prison to test you. You will be persecuted for ten days. Remain faithful even when facing death and I will give you the crown of life an unending, glorious future. Let everyone who can hear, listen to what the spirit is saying to the churches: He who is victorious shall not be hurt by the second death" [when all will be judged by God]. (Revelation 2:9–11)
>
> To Pergamos [third church] Jesus says, "I am fully aware that you live in the city where Satan's throne is, at the center of satanic worship; and yet you remained loyal to me, and refused to deny me, even in the days of Antipas, my faithful witness, was martyred [put to death/killed] among you, where Satan dwells. And yet I have a few things against you. You tolerate some among you

who do as Balaam did when he taught Balak to entice the Israelites to sin by eating food sacrificed to idols and by committing sexual immorality [practice immorality]." (Revelation 2:13–14)

To Thyatira [the fourth church] Jesus says, write, "I am aware of your good deeds your kindness to the poor, your gifts and service to them, also I know your love and faith and patience, and I can see your constant improving in all of these things. Nevertheless, I have this against you: You tolerate that woman Jezebel. She calls herself a prophetess. By her teaching she leads my servants into sexual immorality and the eating of food sacrificed to idols. I have given her time to repent of her immorality, but she is unwilling. So I will cast her on a bed of suffering, and I will make those who commit adultery with her suffer intensely, unless they repent of her ways. I will strike her children dead. Then all the churches will know that I am he who searches hearts and minds, and I will repay each of you according to your deeds. Now I say to the rest of you in Thyaria, to you who do not hold to her teaching and have not learned Satan's so called deep secrets [I will not impose any other burden on you]: Only hold on to what you have until I come. To him who overcomes and does my will to the end, I will give authority [power] over the nations." (Revelation 2:19–26)

To the church in Sardis [fifth church] write, "I know your deeds; you have a reputation of being alive, but you are dead. Wake up [be watchful]! Strengthen what [little] remains and is about to die, for I have not found your deeds complete [perfect] in the sight of my God [your deeds are far from right in the sight of God]. Remember, therefore, what you have received and heard; obey it, and repent. But if you do not wake up [watch], I will come like a thief, and you will not know at what time I will come to you. Yet you have a few people in Sardis who have not soiled their clothes. They will walk with me, dressed in white, for they are worthy. He who overcomes will, like them, be dressed in white. I will never blot out [erase] his name from the book of life, but will acknowledge [confess] his name before my father and his angels [I will announce before my father and his angels that he is mine]. He who has an ear [all who can hear], let him hear what the spirit says to the churches." (Revelation 3:1–6)

To the angel of the church in Philadelphia write: "These are the words of him who is holy and true, who holds the key of David. What he opens no one can shut, and what he shuts no one can open. I know your deeds, I know you well. See, I've placed before you an open door that no one can shut. I know that you have little strength, yet you have kept my word and have not denied my name. I will make those who are the synagogue of Satan, who claim to be Jews though they're not, but are liars, I will make them [I will force them] to come and fall down at your feet and acknowledge that I have loved you. Since you have kept my command to endure patiently [despite the persecution], I will also keep you from the hour of trial [the time of great tribulation and temptation] that is going to, upon the whole world test those who live on the earth. I am coming soon. Hold on to what you have [hold tightly to the little strength you have], so that no one will take your crown. Him who overcomes [conquers] I'll make a pillar in the temple of my God. Never again will he leave it [he will be secure]. I will write on him the name of my God and the name of the city of my God, the new Jerusalem, which is coming down out of heaven from my God; and I will also write on him my new name. He who has an ear, let him hear what the spirit says to the churches." (Revelation 3:7–13)

To the angel of the church in Laodicea write: "These are the words of the Amen, faithful and true witness, the ruler of God's creation. I know your deeds, that you are neither cold nor hot. I wish you were either one or the other! So, because you are lukewarm neither hot nor cold I am about to [I will] spit you out of my mouth. You say, "I'm rich; I've acquired wealth and do not need a thing." but you do not realize that you are wretched, pitiful, poor, blind and naked. I counsel you to buy from me gold refined in the fire, so you can become rich; and have white clothes to wear, so you can cover your shameful nakedness; and salve to put on your eyes, so you can see. Those whom I love I rebuke and discipline. So be earnest, and repent. Here I am! I stand at the door and knock. If anyone hears my voice and opens the door, I will come in and eat with him, and he with me. To him who overcomes, I will give the right to sit with me on my throne, just as I overcame and sat down with my father on his throne. He who has an ear, let him hear what the spirit says to the churches." (Revelation 3:14–22)

# Chapter 5

# The Throne

Then as I looked, I saw a door standing open in heaven! And the voice I'd first heard speaking to me like a trumpet [like a mighty trumpet blast] said, "Come up here, and I will show you what must take place after this [in the future]." At once I was in the spirit, and there before me [Oh the glory of it!] was a throne in heaven with someone sitting on it. And the one who sat there had the appearance of jasper and carelian [great bursts of light flashed forth from him as from a glittering diamond, or from a shining ruby]. A rainbow, resembling an emerald, encircled the throne.

Surrounding the throne were twenty four other thrones [smaller], and seated on them were twenty four elders. They were dressed in white and had crowns of gold on their heads. From the throne came flashes of lightning, rumblings and peals of thunder.

Before the throne, seven lamps were blazing. These are the seven spirits of God [representing the sevenfold spirit of God]. Also before the throne there was what looked like a sea of glass, clear like crystal [shiny crystal sea].

In the center, around the throne, were four living creatures, and they were covered with eyes, in front and in back [stood at the thrones four sides]. The first living creature was like a lion, the second was like an ox, the third had a face like a man, the fourth was like a flying eagle. Each of the four living creatures had six wings and was covered with eyes all around, even under its wings.

Day after day and night after night they never stopped saying: "Holy, holy, holy is the Lord God almighty, the one who was, and is, and is to come." Whenever the living creatures give glory, honor and thanks to him who sits on the throne and who lives forever and ever, the twenty four elders fall down before him who sits on the throne, and worship him who lives forever and ever. They lay there crowns [cast their crowns] before the throne and say: "You are worthy, our Lord and God, to receive glory and honor and power, for you created all things, and by your will they were created and have their being [exist]." (Revelation 4:1–11)

Then I saw in the right hand of him who sat on the throne a scroll with writing on both sides and sealed with seven seals. And I saw a mighty angel proclaiming in a loud voice, "Who is worthy to break the seals and open the scroll?" But no one in heaven or on earth or under the earth could open the scroll or even look inside it. I wept and wept [with disappointment] because no one was found who was worthy to open the scroll or look inside it. Then one of the elders said to me, "Do not weep [stop crying]! See, the lion of the tribe of Judah, the root of David, has triumphed. He is able to open the scroll and its seven seals."

Then I saw a Lamb, looking as if it had been slain [and on the Lamb were wounds that had once caused his death], standing in the center of the throne, encircled by the four living creatures and the elders. He had seven horns and seven eyes, which are the seven spirits of God sent out into all the earth.

He came and took the scroll from the right hand of him who sat on the throne. And when he had taken it, the four living creatures and the twenty four elders fell down before the Lamb.

Each one had a harp and they were holding golden bowls [golden vials] full of incense, the prayers of God's people! And they sang a new song: "You are worthy to take the scroll and to open its seals, because you were slain, and with your blood you purchased men for God from every tribe and language and people and nation. You have made them to be a Kingdom and priests to serve our God, and they will reign on the earth."

Then I looked and heard the voice of many angels, numbering thousands upon thousands, and ten thousand times ten thousand (100 million). They encircled the throne and the living creatures and the elders. In a loud voice they sang: "Worthy is the Lamb, who was slain, to receive power and wealth and wisdom and strength and honor and glory and praise!"

Then I heard every creature in heaven and on earth and under the earth and on the sea, and all that is in them, singing: "To him who sits on the throne and to the Lamb be praise and honor and glory and power, forever and ever!" the four living creatures said, "Amen," and the elders fell down and worshipped. (Revelation 5:1–14)

# Chapter 6

# Only One is Worthy

Be happy if by some illness you die in your sleep tonight, because death tomorrow or the next, will not taste sweet ...

> I watched as the Lamb opened the first of the seven seals. Then I heard one of the four living creatures say in a voice like thunder, "Come!" I looked, and there before me was a white horse! It's rider held a bow, and he was given the crown, and he rode out as a conqueror bent on conquest." (Revelation 6:1–2)

By 2039, China had sealed their reign as the number one exporter in the world, and through careful and gradual transition, it became a self-contained nation, needing nothing from the outside world. For the past forty years China had been buying up the world's exports, leaving the world's reserves extremely low and in return, causing the prices to rise because of supply and demand. Little did the average person know that China had been stockpiling all its imports in huge warehouses all across the nation.

More important, they had been flooding the world market for the past forty years with a million products, from pencils, toys, electronic games, and vehicles, to high-tech computer technology. You might have made it first, but they made it second, and cheaper. They mass-produced each product, paying hardly anything for labor, and flooded the market until as a company you couldn't compete. Lots of companies went out of business in the so-called world recession of 2008. China put on a fake front that they were hurting like the rest of the world, but the key players were laughing and rubbing their hands together in delight as each heavy hitter came crashing down to their knees. Some businesses adapted by closing their factories and buying Chinese products and passing them off as their own. This was a common practice around the world that started in the late 1990s but really took off in 2010.

But the day that matters is January 26, 2043, the Chinese New Year. From that day forward over the next five years, China waged a war far greater than any other war that had come before. China's first direct hit was dropped on the United States of America and delivered a devastating blow to the White House. This was not a chemical warfare bomb or even a conventional bomb; it was the greatest strategic move that China had ever made. It was delivered in a five-ton truck carrying 100 file boxes each weighing twenty-five pounds. It was a lawsuit suing the United States for 20 trillion dollars.

At the forefront of this lawsuit was a cease-and-desist order on import and export trade with the United States delivered to every town, city, state, province, and country of the world along with any known businesses selling or buying from the United States Government. It was much like when a company owes the government taxes and the government sends you the legal papers saying that any monies that you owe this company must be paid to them (the government) and not to the company. If you do pay the company any money after this point, you will be held liable, and now the government can go after you. On top of that, the money you paid the company will not go toward anything you owed them; it kind of just disappears as if to say you were stupid enough to give it to them, and now it's like you never gave it to them in the first place!

The world stood back in shock, and the smart people immediately stopped trading with the United States. The dumb ones felt like this would never stand up in the courts, but after five years in the courtrooms and the trade embargo on the United States, the White House finally caved. It happened only after their own lawyers filed a lawsuit against the government for unpaid lawyers' fees.

*Christ for Life*

Their only choice was to sell off federally and state-owned companies for the fair market value exclusively to the Chinese, per the settlement. This meant that everything from schools, jails, museums, public utilities, to parks and even public bathrooms were now owned by the Chinese government. At first everything seemed the same, but then thousands of Chinese people already living in the States were promoted or hired to key positions in these newly obtained businesses. All at once jails weren't the cushy place of yesterday, but were run streamlined exactly like the one in Arizona. Inmates were forcefully introduced to pink jumpsuits with pink underwear, bag lunches, and Cheerios for breakfast. Nothing was given to them unless they earned it, and that included food and clothing. Shelter became a cot and a tarp-covered shelter under the stars in most states. Supper was no longer provided because it was deemed unnecessary, as the breakfast and lunch rations were more than sufficient for 90 percent of the rest of the world and therefore good enough for the inmates. The state had to pay the jail $35,000 per year, per inmate. Considering all the amenities that were taken away from the prisoners, the Chinese government was able to make a $20,000 profit per inmate each year. At the beginning of 2008, 2.3 million Americans were incarcerated in prisons across the country, and by 2048 the number had increased to 2.9 million. In one year alone, profits from the American prisons came to $58 billion.

Public schools had cost an average of $11,000 per student, running an expense of more than $500 billion a year. Again with a few cost-cutting measures, the Chinese government profited another $47 billion from American public schools in the first year.

At first American citizens seemed like they were on the edge of an all-out war, but the Chinese government did something that no American president had ever been able to do. They managed to improve each school's quality of education and provide a more stable and safe environment for the students. In addition, American incarceration levels decreased by almost a million people in the first year, saving taxpayers $35 billion. To save face with the American taxpayer, the US government immediately put this money into the universal health care program to provide care for low-income families. As an act of goodwill, the Chinese government gave a onetime $90 billion donation to the same program the following day. These key factors kept the peace between angry Americans and their new big brother, China.

As for the rest of the world, they weren't so lucky. In 2049 the Chinese government filed more than 2,000 lawsuits against countries, provinces, and large companies known to have traded with the United States during their five-year legal battle. Countries and companies hit hardest by the lawsuit were all Mexican and Canadian owned, as they thought there was no way the United States would back down. Many of the poor countries of Africa and elsewhere out of necessity refused to stop trading with the United States. Little did anyone know that China forgave 100 billion dollars in debt in exchange for a settlement and the names of all the companies and countries they had had dealings with in the past five years. China already had the names and most of the amounts of the transactions, but it was a source of great amusement to make the Americans squirm after being caught in lie after lie about each trade they had done after the lawsuit was filed.

The lawsuits ranged from a hundred thousand dollars to upwards of two billion dollars. Many were settled with companies having to go into foreclosure, accounting for ninety well-known international companies being taken over and run by the Chinese. China vowed to make an example of any country or company that did not settle with them within the year. On the second-to-last day before an example was to be made, Canada and Mexico settled with China. They signed over full control of all provincial and federally run prisons as well as public schools and all utilities such as natural gas, electricity, and water. Everyone expected the Chinese government to give a sizable donation back to these governments' health care systems at the end of 2050. It never did, and you could tell a storm was coming, and everyone knew that blood was in the air.

> "When the Lamb opened the second seal, I heard the second living creatures say, 'come!' Then another horse came out, a fiery red one. Its rider was given power to take peace from the earth and to make men slay each other. To him was given a large sword." (Revelation 6:3–4)

In the first couple of months of 2051, riots began all over Mexico to protest the flood of Chinese people taking all the school-teaching and prison-guard jobs. Two days later, riots broke out in Montreal and Toronto, in Canada. By the end of the week, there were riots in every major city in Canada. By the end of March, more than 2,000 Chinese civilians had been murdered in Canada and Mexico. During this time the Chinese shut down or sabotaged every service such as the Internet, cable TV, phones, and cell phones. They even controlled all the newspapers and refused to print a paper during this time. As a last resort in the last week of March, the Chinese government turned off all the utilities such as water, natural gas, and electricity, which in turn brought the cities to a standstill as people even ran out of gasoline for their vehicles. Canada, Mexico, and even the United States were all affected as Big Brother had proof that Americans were helping the Canadian and Mexican rioters.

Some will tell you that what happened next was in retaliation for the riots, but others will tell you that it was planned all along. On April 1, 2051, the Chinese government simultaneously deployed fifty-five nuclear bombs. The first one hit Vancouver, British Columbia, at 3:59 a.m. and the second moments later. For the next twenty minutes, forty-nine more nuclear bombs fell on sixteen of the most densely populated cities in Canada. At 4:24 a.m., three nuclear bombs fell on the city of Toronto, and the last of them hit the International Peace Gardens on the US/Canadian border at 4:27 a.m. Almost 3,800,000 Canadians were suspected to have died within a week of the nuclear attacks based on the evidence collected from the bombing of Hiroshima in 1945, and it was also suspected that within five years the death toll would rise to 7,600,000.

A survivor described the damage to people:

> The appearance of people was ... well, they all had skin blackened by burns ... They had no hair because their hair was burned. At a glance you couldn't tell whether you were looking at them from in front or in back ... They held their arms bent [forward] like this ... and their skin—not only on their hands, but on their faces and bodies, too—hung down ... If there had been only one or two such people ... perhaps I would not have had such

a strong impression. But wherever I walked, I met these people ... Many of them died along the road—I can still picture them in my mind—like walking ghosts. (**See appendix.)

Mexico woke up at 5:07 a.m. on April 1, 2051, to the sounds of heavy artillery shells crashing down into practically every building along the coastline. Forty-five Chinese destroyers were staggered in the ocean bent on revenge of the deaths of the 2,000 Chinese who had died at the hands of the Mexican and Canadian rioters. The shelling went on for an hour until Mexican citizens flocked to the shoreline waving anything they could find that was white. Some waved shirts, socks, or simply white pieces of paper in the air. All they wanted was for the shelling to stop, and at 6:07 a.m., it did, but not until 90 percent of the coastline was reduced to rubble and 80,000 people were dead. Within four hours of the initial attack, 45,000 Chinese soldiers were occupying the coastline of Mexico. Every hour thousands upon thousands of Chinese soldiers made their way off the ships and onto the Mexican shoreline.

Each day the Chinese soldiers pushed resisters farther and farther back toward the US border. After three weeks the Chinese army stopped just one mile from the US border so that within that one mile, an estimated 200,000 rioting Mexicans were trapped between the Chinese army and the US Border Patrol. As the Mexicans tried to cross the US border, the Americans opened up their guns into the dirt inches away from the Mexicans stuck between a rock and a hard place. A few were shot at by the border patrol to push them back. The Chinese army was immediately ordered to open fire, sparing no one, and 40,000 Mexicans died within that one mile. The Mexicans ran for their lives toward the hundred or so border patrol guards and extra security. The Americans managed to kill a few more Mexicans but were quickly overrun by the stampede of fleeing people. The Mexicans jumped the border crossing, taking their guns with them into the United States.

So now what will become of 160,000 Mexicans fleeing Mexico in a country filled with gun-toting Americans who despise Mexican illegal aliens no matter what the excuse?

# Chapter 7

# 𝔄 Loaf of 𝔅read

"When the Lamb opened the third seal, I heard the third living creature say, 'Come!' I looked, and there before me was a black horse! Its rider was holding a pair of scales in his hand. Then I heard what sounded like a voice among the four living creatures, saying, 'A quart of wheat for a day's wages (denarius\*\*\* see appendix), and three quarts of barley for a day's wages and do not damage the oil and the wine!'" Revelation 6:6

## Why

Why does God allow people to be homeless
Why does he let people steal whatever they want
Why does God allow people to be raped
Why does he allow people to starve to death
Why does God allow genocide
Why doesn't he stop all these things
Why won't God do anything

*Scott Ballentyne*

The real question is why won't we

God has done something
He gave you and me a brain to rationalize with
God gave us a conscience to know right from wrong
He gave us the Bible to tell us right from wrong just in case anyone tried to say they didn't know the difference

God provided us with the means to feed ourselves
He gave us the means to provide shelter for ourselves
God gave us the means to protect ourselves

*Us* does not mean me and only me, or me and my family
It doesn't mean me and my country, or me and the more fortunate
It means all of us as a world, for that matter all of God's creations
Every human that ever was, and ever is to be
Jesus died for all of us, not just me

We are the ones who choose to do nothing, not God
Remember, doing hardly nothing is closer to nothing than it is to really doing something

We could feed the whole world if we wanted to
Every single person could have a home
We could protect every nation, even if they didn't have oil or something else that we wanted from them
We have the means to teach every person to read, write, and speak their chosen language
I don't want to be forced to speak French any more than a French person wants to be forced to learn English

We have the means to make universal laws
More important, we have the means to enforce those laws

We are so worried about a criminal's rights that we forget about our greater priority
Which is to protect everyone else's rights from the criminals

*Christ for Life*

When Jesus comes to rule for a thousand years on earth do you really think there will be homeless or starving people
Do you think when people commit crimes, Jesus will say, "They didn't know better"
Criminals and other bad people will be dealt with harshly. Otherwise, why would the Bible say that Jesus will rule with a rod of iron

Do not fool yourselves
Jesus is full of love and mercy
But with that comes justice and punishment
After all he is his father's son

Even after Jesus rules for a thousand years, there will be many that will be swayed against him
The number that rise against him will be so great that in the Bible it is compared to the grains of sand in the sea
After a thousand years has passed, Jesus will deal with them harshly and throw them into the burning lake of fire, and there they will experience a second death

Which side will you be on
If you are not for me, then you are against me
If you don't pick a side to stand up for, you're still ultimately against him
"How I wish that you were either cold or hot, but because you are lukewarm I will spew you from my mouth"
God seems to have more contempt for those who do nothing than those who at least pick a side
God gave us the means to take care of ourselves
In our country we have the ability to choose a leader who best suits what we want them to accomplish
So let's start supporting those who want to make a positive difference
Let's support those who want to protect the citizens and punish the criminals

God empowered all of us to protect all his children
Not just the ones we choose to say are worthy

Remember, it's not God who's not doing his part
It's us, and this time it does mean me but it also means you

Nick King, of the band Thirty Two, had honorable intentions when over the course of fifteen years he lobbied the governments, churches, and any celebrity who would listen that we were responsible for feeding the hungry people of the world. The slogan used was "We are the ones who allow the children to starve." With this truth ringing in our ears, every nation by 2040 took the necessary steps to provide food and water to every person on the planet. I myself embraced this vision and did all I could to see it fulfilled. We did not see that no good deed goes unpunished by Satan.

Between 2017 and 2023, the food industry had become one of the fastest-growing markets in the world's history. With the supply and demand of countries like China and Indonesia, the World Grain Reserves, which were at fifty-three days in 2008, were down to six days on April 5, 2051. Many watchdogs have been accusing China of hoarding reserves of wheat, barley, rice, and other sources of food for the past forty years. On top of that, the global consumption rose tenfold, since the ways of the Western world have been embraced by practically the whole world except the Muslim nation. The "Feed the Nations" campaign that Nick spearheaded has been blamed for as much as 50 percent in the drop in reserves, but many suspect that China's hoarding was to blame for much of the rest. The fact that China destroyed so much of the Canadian and Mexican landscape during the attacks a few days earlier didn't help either, considering Canada was a major exporter of grain until then. At the current rate of decline, it was projected that by winter, the grain reserves would be all used up and that roughly 500 million people of all walks of life would die in the coming year alone if drastic measures weren't taken to prevent it from happening.

This drove the price of food to unheard-of prices in Canada: $100 for a loaf of bread, $70 for a jug of milk, $125 per pound of beef. Ninety-nine percent of the world's people could no longer afford to eat. Now it was our turn to finally feel how the rest of the world felt when they went to bed starving. How long would it take before we made mud pies to try to trick our minds into thinking there was food in our stomachs? How long would it take before we Canadians looked like the starving children of Africa?

The only people on the bottom who made it through these times were the ones who banded together. Middle-class families became the working poor, and minimum-wage laborers were forced to beg on the streets or band together with a middle-class family or friend. Our 1,400-square-foot house in the North End of Winnipeg that used to have a maximum of two adults and a few children had up to eighty people at one time just to pay the bills of one household. It didn't do much good to beg, because most people didn't have two nickels to rub together, never mind a penny for a beggar. If a person smoked or drank, every luxury came at the cost of having less food. Every child was looked at as another mouth to be fed, and many children were forced to drop out of school and work just so they could eat. Otherwise if you had children, whether or not they ate was determined by whether or not you ate.

> "When the Lamb opened the fourth seal, I heard the voice of the fourth living creature say, 'Come!' I looked and there before me was a pale horse! Its rider was named Death, and Hades was following close behind him. They were given power over a fourth of the earth to kill by sword, famine and plague, and by the wild beasts of the earth." (Revelation 6:7–8)

The days after the announcement of how low the world's grain supplies had fallen were filled with mass hysteria, and hoarding happened almost immediately around the globe. At first people bought what they could, but more and more under the cover of darkness, stores were robbed, not of their money but of their food. Many people stopped going to work and just stole full time. Why go to work when they didn't earn enough to survive on what they made? Instead, normally law-abiding citizens resorted to armed robbery. It would be bizarre to say the least to see your next door neighbor at your door with a pistol to your head, demanding all your food while his wife and kids ransacked your house. After all, the two of you had just played a round of golf together last fall, and his kids were over in the summer, swimming in your pool. None of that matters to them now. They're like coke addicts doing lines off the toilet tank at the bar. You have no idea why they're doing it; all you know is that they are.

With the shortage of food, many well-meaning pet owners released their pets into the streets. However, others were desperate and ate their own pets, and many others hunted wildlife or stray animals. Places such as zoos, farms, and even aquariums became big targets for hungry or just ruthless people. Once again some zookeepers and farmers released the caged animals to give them at least a fighting chance. Granted, what chance did a cow have? But an angry bull, on the other hand—he had a chance. The lions, tigers, and such released from the zoos—they had a chance. The dogs and people who hunted together in a pack—they had a chance.

During this time many people died from the brutality of the situation, and others died from starvation and plagues. Within a year, more than 2 billion people from all walks of life were believed to be dead. All forms of government or unity were lost faster than rats trying to flee the *Titanic*. That was one thing that was not in decline … rats. Quickly rumor spread that there were more rats and mice than people alive on the planet and that they were spreading disease like wildfire. Things like the black plague, mad cow, SARS, the bird flu, and any other disease that had come our way in the last two hundred years was back with a vengeance with no sign of stopping.

I watched as a man running for his life was attacked by a pack of wild dogs. I envisioned those dogs dragging his soul to hell while he died. They wouldn't even wait for his last breath.

> "When he opened the fifth seal, I saw under the altar the souls of those who had been slain because of the word of God and the testimony they had maintained. They called out in a loud voice, "How long, Sovereign Lord, holy and true, until you judge the inhabitants of the earth and avenge our blood?" Then each of them was given a white

robe, and they were told to wait a little longer, until the number of their fellow servants and brothers who were to be killed as they had been was complete." (Revelation 6:9–11)

People seemed to brush aside the fact that China just committed the biggest atrocity in the world's history, because right now they cared more about whether or not they were going to be able to eat. Instead they seemed to focus their anger in a different direction. Many nonbelievers come to faith in times of crisis. But as many as come, there are as many who look for something or someone to lash out at to get some kind of revenge for what has happened. This was a very trying time for new and old believers alike. Many believers, swayed by their anger toward God, turned on their own kind. Many turned against God out of fear of persecution by nonbelievers. Believers started to be killed all over the world just days after the initial broadcast about the food shortage. Many radicals burned churches and homes of Christian and Jewish believers. They were not the only churches or believers to be targeted, but they most definitely suffered the most casualties. Some people danced in the streets like they did on September 11, 2001, as the World Trade Center collapsed.

Somehow I'm reminded of the movie *The Kingdom,* which is about terrorism, when the main American female character is crying and the male character whispers to her and she stops crying. You wonder what he said to her, but you kind of forget about it until a similar circumstance happens towards the end of the movie: an older Muslim man is dying after being shot by the infidels and he whispers to a small Muslim boy who is crying, and at that moment the boy stops. Only then is it revealed what each man said: "We will not rest until every last one of them is dead."

Many conflicts in the past were of people of one religion fighting those of another religion, but this wasn't about Muslims against Christians. It was about nonbelievers and former believers lashing out against God, any God, and any person or thing that represented a God. Just like witches were burned at the stake hundreds of years ago, many believers were burned alive. Self-appointed cleanup crews burned the bodies of the ones who were killed wherever they lay. In many cases they would simply burn the person's house down with them inside it. They said they were doing "God's work and preventing the spread of disease" as they cackled and poured the gasoline.

A nine-year-old boy is playing with a lighter he found. Flick, and the flame is hot. He lets go of the button and the flame is out. He raises the bottle of hairspray he stole from his sister's room and sprays it as the lighter flicks once more. A ball of flame shoots out from the can with all the splendor of a fire breather at the circus. The boy is amazed at the beauty and the power he now holds. He smiles a sinister smile as he lowers the aim of the flame onto his victim, a helpless cat. He stops the flame for a moment, only to spray the cat down with the hairspray from head to toe. The cat's owner catches the boy as he lights the hairspray one last time to bring his completed joy to an end.

The man, six feet tall, screams his fury, and the boy fears for his life. The boy drops his tools of torture and runs to his house, locks the door, and runs to his room in the basement. He shakes with fear and screams as he hears the front door being kicked in by the pursuing man. The boy screams and screams like he's about to be murdered, with the intensity of that little girl last year whose mother wouldn't let her have her way at the mall. She screamed holy terror so that everyone at the mall would think the mother was about to kill her right there in the center of the mall with a hundred witnesses watching. The boy can hear the man's footsteps coming down the stairs and screams again, but this time he screams, "I'm sorry, I'm sorry, please forgive me for what I have done! Please don't hit me, Daddy!"

These are the sick and twisted times that are already here but will only be magnified in the coming days.

# Chapter 8

# Be Warned

For months after the nuclear attacks, many people around the world gave reports of earthquake tremors at all hours of the day and night. Finally a big one hit at noon on July 18, 2051. A great earthquake unlike any other ever measured in Canada happened in, of all places, Winnipeg, Manitoba. An earthquake had never struck there before and was directly attributed to the nuclear attacks. The earthquake split a giant crater two blocks wide, right in the center of downtown, spewing out what seemed like dark black ash. The ash seemed to go for miles and miles up into the sky, never stopping, and started to block out the sun. The ground trembled again greatly and then the whole earth itself was said to have shook violently.

When I looked around, nothing could be seen, as the ash had now completely blotted out the sun. It was pointless trying to move anywhere, because anywhere I moved, I stumbled over rubble or dead bodies. People were screaming and screaming to the point that I fired my gun in their direction until they stopped. After that all you heard was people crying, some praying to God for forgiveness, others praying for it to end. I even started to cry, praying for my family, for my own forgiveness.

Many hours later, at a time that seemed like night, the moon seemed blood red, and many people started screaming again for God to kill them, because they didn't want to live in this kind of a world anymore. He must have heard their prayers, or mine for them to stop screaming, because I heard a building crash and the screaming stopped. Then it seemed to get hotter and hotter, and the wind didn't move. The ash just seemed to be suspended in air, not moving here or there. "Oh, God, why didn't you take me?" That's what I asked God for three days while I waited for the ash to subside so I could see enough to walk one step, never mind find my way home. If home was even there anymore. No one could deny God's awesome power.

> I watched as he opened the sixth seal. There was a great earthquake. The sun turned black like sackcloth made of goat hair, the whole moon turned blood red, and the stars in the sky fell to the earth, as late figs drop from a fig tree when shaken by a strong wind. The sky receded like a scroll, rolling up, and every mountain and island was removed from its place.
>
> Then the kings of the earth, the princes, the generals, the rich, the mighty, and even the slave and every free man hid in caves and among the rocks of the mountains. They called to the mountains and the rocks, "Fall on us and hide us from the face of him who sits on the throne and from the wrath of the Lamb! For the day of their wrath has come, and who can stand?" (Revelation 6:12–17)
>
> After this I saw four angels standing at the four corners of the earth, holding back the four winds of the earth to prevent any wind from blowing on the land or on the sea or on any tree. Then I saw another angel coming up from the east, having the seal of the living God. He called out in a loud voice to the four angels who had been given power to harm the land and the sea: "Do not harm the land or the sea or the trees until we put a seal on the foreheads of the servants of our God." Then I heard the number of those who were sealed: 144,000 from all the tribes of Israel.
>
> From the tribe of Judah 12,000 were sealed, from the tribe of Reuben 12,000, from the tribe of Gad 12,000, from the tribe of Asher 12,000, from the tribe of Naphtali 12,000, from the tribe of Manasseh 12,000, from the tribe of Simeon 12,000, from the tribe of Levi 12,000, from the tribe of Issachar 12,000, from the tribe of Zebulun

12,000, from the tribe of Joseph 12,000, from the tribe of Benjamin 12,000.

After this I looked and there before me was a great multitude that no one could count, from every nation, tribe, people and language, standing before the throne and in front of the Lamb. They were wearing white robes and were holding palm branches in their hands. And they cried out in a loud voice: "Salvation belongs to our God, who sits on the throne, and to the Lamb." All the angels were standing around the throne and around the elders and the four living creatures. They fell down on their faces before the throne and worshiped God, saying: "Amen! Praise and glory and wisdom and thanks and honor and power and strength be to our God forever and ever. Amen!"

Then one of the elders asked me, "These in white robes—who are they, and where did they come from?" I answered, "Sir, you know." And he said, "These are they who have come out of the great tribulation; they have washed their robes and made them white in the blood of the Lamb. Therefore, "they are before the throne of God and serve him day and night in his temple; and he who sits on the throne will spread his tent over them. Never again will they hunger; never again will they thirst. The sun will not beat upon them, nor any scorching heat. For the Lamb at the center of the throne will be their shepherd; he will lead them to springs of living water. And God will wipe away every tear from their eyes." (Revelation 7:1–17)

Now, brothers, about times and dates we do not need to write to you, for you know very well that the day of the Lord will come like a thief in the night. While people are saying, "Peace and safety," destruction will come on them suddenly, as labor pains on a pregnant woman, and they will not escape. But you, brothers, are not in darkness so that this day should surprise you like a thief. You are all sons of the light and sons of the day. We do not belong to the night or to the darkness. So then, let us not be like others, who are asleep, but let us be alert and self-controlled. For those who sleep, sleep at night, and those who get drunk, get drunk at night. But since we belong to the day, let us be self-controlled, putting on faith and love as a breastplate, and the hope of salvation as a helmet. For God did not appoint us to suffer wrath but to receive salvation through our Lord Jesus Christ. He died for us so that, whether we are awake or asleep, we may live together with him. Therefore encourage one another and build each other up, just as in fact you are doing.

Final Instructions

Now we ask you, brothers, to respect those who work hard among you, who are over you in the Lord and who admonish you. Hold them in the highest regard in love because of their work. Live in peace with each other. And we urge you, brothers, warn those who are idle, encourage the timid, help the weak, be patient with everyone. Make sure that nobody pays back wrong for wrong, but always try to be kind to each other and to everyone else. Be joyful always; pray continually; give thanks in all circumstances, for this is God's will for you in Christ Jesus. Do not put out the Spirit's fire; do not treat prophecies with contempt. Test everything. Hold on to the good. Avoid every kind of evil. May God himself, the God of peace, sanctify you through and through. May your whole spirit, soul and body be kept blameless at the coming of our Lord Jesus Christ. The one who calls you is faithful and he will do it. Brothers, pray for us. Greet all the brothers with a holy kiss. I charge you before the Lord to have this letter read to all the brothers. The grace of our Lord Jesus Christ be with you. (1 Thessalonians 5)

When he opened the seventh seal, there was silence in heaven for about half an hour. And I saw the seven angels who stand before God, and to them were given seven trumpets. Another angel, who had a golden censer, came and stood at the altar. He was given much incense to offer, with the prayers of all the saints, on the golden altar before the throne. The smoke of the incense, together with the prayers of the saints, went up before God from the angel's hand. Then the angel took the censer, filled it with fire from the altar, and hurled it on the earth; and there came peals of thunder, rumblings, flashes of lightning and an earthquake. (Revelation 8:1–5)

Signs of the End of the Age

Jesus left the temple and was walking away when his disciples came up to him to call his attention to its buildings. "Do you see all these things?" he asked. "I tell you the truth, not one stone here will be left on another; every one will be thrown down." As Jesus was sitting on the Mount of Olives, the disciples came to him privately. "Tell us," they said, "when will this happen, and what will be the sign of your coming and of the end of the age?" Jesus answered: "Watch out that no one deceives you. For many will come in my name, claiming, 'I am the Christ,' and will deceive many. You will hear of wars and rumors of wars, but see to it that you are not alarmed. Such things must happen, but the end is still to come. Nation will rise against nation, and kingdom against kingdom. There will be famines and earthquakes in various places. All these are the beginning of birth pains.

"Then you will be handed over to be persecuted and put to death, and you will be hated by all nations because of me. At that time many will turn away from the faith and will betray and hate each other, and many false prophets will appear and deceive many people. Because of the increase of wickedness, the love of most will grow cold, but he who stands firm to the end will be saved. And this gospel of the kingdom will be preached in the whole world as a testimony to all nations, and then the end will come.

"So when you see standing in the holy place 'the abomination that causes desolation,' spoken of through the prophet Daniel—let the reader understand—then let those who are in Judea flee to the mountains. Let no one on the roof of his house go down to take anything out of the house. Let no one in the field go back to get his cloak. How dreadful it will be in those days for pregnant women and nursing mothers! Pray that your flight will not take place in winter or on the Sabbath. For then there will be great distress, unequaled from the beginning of the world until now—and never to be equaled again. If those days had not been cut short, no one would survive, but for the sake of the elect those days will be shortened. At that time if anyone says to you, 'Look, here is the Christ!' or, 'There he is!' do not believe it. For false Christs and false prophets will appear and perform great signs and miracles to deceive even the elect—if that were possible. See, I have told you ahead of time.

"So if anyone tells you, 'There he is, out in the desert,' do not go out; or, 'Here he is, in the inner rooms,' do not believe it. For as lightning that comes from the east is visible even in the west, so will be the coming of the Son of Man. Wherever there is a carcass, there the vultures will gather. Immediately after the distress of those days 'the sun will be darkened, and the moon will not give its light; the stars will fall from the sky, and the heavenly bodies will be shaken.' At that time the sign of the Son of Man will appear in the sky, and all the nations of the earth will mourn. They will see the Son of Man coming on the clouds of the sky, with power and great glory. And he will send his angels with a loud trumpet call, and they will gather his elect from the four winds, from one end of the heavens to the other. Now learn this lesson from the fig tree: As soon as its twigs get tender and its leaves come out, you know that summer is near. Even so, when you see all these things, you know that it is near, right at the door. I tell you the truth, this generation will certainly not pass away until all these things have happened. Heaven and earth will pass away, but my words will never pass away."

The Day and Hour Unknown

"No one knows about that day or hour, not even the angels in heaven, nor the Son, but only the Father. As it was in the days of Noah, so it will be at the coming of the Son of Man. For in the days before the flood, people were eating and drinking, marrying and giving in marriage, up to the day Noah entered the ark; and they knew nothing about what would happen until the flood came and took them all away. That is how it will be at the coming of the Son of Man. Two men will be in the field; one will be taken and the other left. Two women will be grinding with a hand mill; one will be taken and the other left.

"Therefore keep watch, because you do not know on what day your Lord will come. But understand this: If the owner of the house had known at what time of night the thief was coming, he would have kept watch and would not have let his house be broken into. So you also must be ready, because the Son of Man will come at an hour when you do not expect him. Who then is the faithful and wise servant, whom the master has put in charge of the servants in his household to give them their food at the proper time? It will be good for that servant whose master finds him doing so when he returns. I tell you the truth, he will put him in charge of all his possessions. But suppose that servant is wicked and says to himself, 'My master is staying away a long time,' and he then begins to beat his fellow servants and to eat and drink with drunkards.

The master of that servant will come on a day when he does not expect him and at an hour he is not aware of. He will cut him to pieces and assign him a place with the hypocrites, where there will be weeping and gnashing of teeth." (Matthew 24)

After a few days the ash finally subsided from the great earthquake and I was slowly able to make my way home. Word reached us that the United States White House had collapsed in the great world earthquake and that the president and vice president were both killed in the destruction. I wondered what kind of man would even put his name on the ballot to clean up a mess like this one. President Brad Olson had put his name in at the most inopportune time forty years ago and was bogged down by the so-called global recession. He wasn't able to shine the way I and others had hoped he would be able to. He had been just a blip on the radar, but maybe that had been the plan all along. I couldn't imagine who it was going to be. Who would want to lead the United States in its darkest hour?

# Chapter 9

# 𝔉𝔞𝔩𝔩𝔦𝔫𝔤

(Please note that pages 51 to 61 and pages 66 to 69 are purposely repeated from chapter 1 and 2 as to stay in the timeline)

Monday, July 31, 2051

The global population is in steady decline after a series of catastrophic events, including the recent attacks on Canada and Mexico. It is estimated that in the last three months, billions of people around the world have died from wars, starvation, or religious persecution. Today when I turned on the television, all I could see was death and destruction on every channel. The Arab nations of Pakistan, Iran, and Iraq were being blamed for releasing some sort of chemical weapon over Israel that was believed to have killed well over a hundred thousand Jews who lived there. One man dared to give an exact number. He said, "The number is one hundred and forty-four thousand, and with that the fate of the world is sealed."

I thought to myself, *That number sounds familiar,* and at just that moment, all the power went out in my house—well, if you could still call it a house. It was barely standing after the recent earthquake. I was sure that as soon as the structural engineers came next week, they would deem it unsafe and book it for demolishing. Then what?

I gave my head a shake to get back into reality. It was light outside, so I could see the front street clearly since the blinds were open. It was quite odd, I thought—the message of the 144,000, I mean, not the light. I looked at my watch. It was 7:00 a.m. I went to the fridge and pulled out the milk. I sat down, poured myself a bowl of cereal, and contemplated shooting myself right there at the kitchen table. My gun was within reach, so it would hardly take any effort. I wouldn't even have to get up.

I thought to myself, *Why did we go visit my friend Janice in Wawanesa the first weekend of April? Why did the van break down so that we had to stay there for a week waiting for parts? I wish I had been in Winnipeg and that the nuclear bomb had landed square on my head. At least I wouldn't be here still trying to pick up the pieces months later, only to be followed by an earthquake. Really, an earthquake? We live in excuse my French, Winnipeg, not in San Francisco. We're not supposed to have earthquakes here!*

Just then my nine-year-old son, Stephan, came up from behind me and said, "Love you, Declan. What's for breakfast?"

"Cereal," I said as I pulled the gun toward me. "Go wake up the clan for me, will you?"

It was more of a telling than an asking, and he knew it.

With that, he yelled at the top of his lungs, "Get up, you lazy buggers." I looked at him and rolled my eyes. He shrugged and said, "What? Did you want me to go wake eighty people up one by one like Mom would do?"

Stephan had become my son by marriage but also by choice, just like his sisters, Amelia and Amanda, who were now seventeen and sixteen. My biological son, Colin, had gone back home to his mother's yesterday, like he did every Sunday night for the week until I picked him up on Friday again.

"No," I said. How could I blame him? I was about to wake them up with a gunshot. His way was definitely a lot less messy. Eighty people. I can't believe eighty people even fit in my house, never mind that I would "let" them in. Since the food shortage, though, what was I supposed to do, let my friends and neighbors starve to death? Ask me now and I'd say yes! Let them all starve, they drive me crazy!

"Oh," I said. "Love you too, Stephan."

As the "clan" filtered in, I zoned out and turned on my mp3 radio as I walked out the front door. The reception seemed very fuzzy. I checked the time: 7:32 a.m. A girl giving the daily news said, "There seems to be a province-wide power outage, and the only reason we're able to broadcast is because of the backup generators we have. It also seems like the power outage might be more widespread and that for now, all flights are cancelled to and from anywhere in the country."

She went on to say, "The Manitoba government tells us that we should expect it to be months before uninterrupted power can be expected, considering the damage from the earthquake and all the rubble that has to be cleaned up before workers can access all the downed power lines and blown transformers."

I got to work a couple of hours later. You never realize how far away somewhere is until you have to walk there. My boss, Jeff, was already there with both overhead doors opened up. "The power is out, and I couldn't see inside unless I opened the doors," he told me.

I just nodded and walked inside. We talked for a bit like we always did, and I asked him if I could use the work van for personal use because mine had been written off after a tree fell on it during the earthquake. I knew it wouldn't be a problem, but I still asked. When I went to leave the shop to start my day, the van wouldn't start. I tried ten times to get it to start, but it wouldn't turn over. "Eish. Stupid alternator," I muttered. The alternator had been going for the past two months. I carried a new one with me in the van because we knew it was going to fail eventually. I got out and removed the new alternator from the box and proceeded to get some of the tools I needed. My boss popped the hood for me and guided me through the process of removing the old alternator. Two hours later, we finally had the alternator in—*we* meaning me. I cleaned up a little as Jeff got in the driver's seat and tried to start the van. Still the van wouldn't start.

"Beautiful day. I guess we'll have to get it towed." I said.

I picked up the phone, but it was dead. I put it back, opened my cell phone, dialed the number, and hit "send," but nothing happened. It just kept searching for a signal. "Jeff, try your cell. I can't get a signal." I walked outside to see if I could get a better signal. I noticed out on the front street that there were no cars going by, even though it was normally quite busy. Instead there were a few vehicles parked with the doors wide open and their occupants outside trying to use their cell phones with no luck either, it seemed. "Do you have a signal, Jeff?" I asked.

"No" was his only reply.

I walked to the front street and looked down in both directions. Nothing was moving. As far as I could see, there were just dead cars with people standing around trying to use their cell phones. I heard a dull noise getting louder. At first I couldn't make it out, but then it became clearer and closer. It was screaming. In the distance, from the south, I could see people running and screaming, but seconds after they started running, I saw them falling. As their lifeless bodies dropped to the ground, a man behind me screamed, "Cover your mouth. It's probably an airborne chemical!" and with that he too fell to the ground. My head started to feel light. I tried to run, but I could feel myself falling, and my eyes slowly closed. The last thing I saw was my watch flashing in front of my face: 1:00 p.m. July 31, 1:00 p.m. July 31, 1:00 p.m. July 31.

# Chapter 10

# 𝔚𝔞𝔨𝔢 𝔘𝔭

(Please note that pages 51 to 61 and pages 66 to 69 are purposely repeated from chapter 1 and 2 as to stay in the timeline)

*Wake up, wake up, wake up,* I kept telling myself. *Wake up!* Slowly I opened my eyes. All I could see were white lines. I rubbed my eyes and finally notice how uncomfortable I was. I stretched and creaked as my neck and back cracked back into place. I opened my eyes once again to see the white lines in front of my face. I lifted my head a little and saw the asphalt, and then it dawned on me where I was. I was still on the road. I stood up and looked around; the cars were still all around, and cell phones lay here and there on the ground. There were still lots of people lying on the ground, and only about half of them were moving around.

I looked at my watch, which was now flashing 3:00 p.m. It seemed as though whatever had happened, I had been out for a couple of hours and so had everyone else. I was groggy, but I walked back over to the shop and called out for Jeff. "Jeff? Jeff? Where are you?" I checked under and in the van we had been working on and didn't find him. Still I called out his name. "Jeff, it isn't funny anymore!" I walked upstairs, but he wasn't up there either. I went back down and looked around some more. Both the work vans were still there, and so was Jeff's Hummer. I pulled out my cell phone and called his number, and it started to ring. I took the phone away from my ear and could hear his phone ringing somewhere in the shop. Finally I pinpointed it. It seemed to be coming from the bathroom. I called out to him, but again he never answered. I closed my cell phone and the ringing stopped. I unlocked the bathroom and saw Jeff lying on the floor.

"Wake up, Jeff, wake up." He didn't move. "Jeff! Wake up! Come on, man, you have to get up!" I knelt down, and I couldn't hear him breathing. Jeff had a condition called sleep apnea, which meant that he sometimes stopped breathing while he slept. I leaned in really close, listening with my left ear since I'm practically deaf in my right. Closer still I leaned in up to his mouth, but I couldn't hear or feel a thing. I touched his face with my hand. It was cold. I opened his eyes, but I could see that he was already gone. I pulled at his legs to straighten his body out and noticed it didn't want to straighten out like a limp body would normally. His body seemed stiff. I knelt down again and tried to do CPR for a few minutes. I knew it was hopeless, but part of me wanted to believe he wasn't dead. The logical side of me knew he had been dead for a couple of hours and that nobody could have saved him. Nobody could have saved any of them.

Just then my cell phone rang. ICE is the name that came up, 867-5309. ICE stands for "in case of emergency," a.k.a. my home phone number. "Hello," I said as I answered it, expecting it to be my wife, Marie.

"Hello," she said. "Your wife is dead." Then I realized it wasn't Marie. It was her sister Lori. Her sister was never one to mince words and just told it how it was, but this was over the top.

"What do you mean?" I asked as I felt the tears well up in my eyes. The shock made me sit down.

"I mean she's dead, stiff, not moving, not breathing, cold and all that—dead. So are your mom and Stephan, Ethan, and my mom and dad too. Along with everyone else who was at home when it happened." Then she said, "Check your watch, check your phone. What time does it say?"

I could already tell it was a loaded question, but I looked anyway. "3:10 p.m. Why?"

"And what time was it before you were knocked out?" she asked.

How did she know that had happened to me? With that, the bottom fell out from my stomach, and I felt tears roll down my cheeks. I choked on my emotions as I said, "One."

For the first time ever in the five years I had known Lori, I could hear her crying on the phone. "It happened here at 1:00 p.m., too. You have to come home, Declan."

*Christ for Life*

Since the food shortage, Lori and her boyfriend, Ethan, my mother-in-law and father-in-law, my mom, as well as seventy other people had been living at our house because nobody could make ends meet on their own. It cost your left leg just to feed yourself, never mind to pay for rent or a mortgage. "You have to come home, Declan. I haven't heard from the girls either." The girls (Amelia and Amanda) would have been at school when it happened.

"Okay, I know. I'll be right there in fifteen minutes," I said. I hung up my phone, went over to my work van, inserted the key into the ignition, and turned the key. Just like I expected, it started. I turned it back off and got out of the van. I had an eerie feeling that the van not starting and all the stalled vehicles outside was God performing "controlled chaos." Before I closed the door to the shop and locked it, I yelled out one more time, "Jeff!" I wished so much that he would respond, but I knew he wouldn't answer, and he didn't. I grabbed the keys to his Hummer and locked the shop door. I wasn't going to take the van when I could take the Hummer, that's for sure.

It was a little more difficult than you might think, driving home, because there were still quite a few vehicles abandoned all over the road. It was like swerving around cones on an obstacle course but these were cars and trucks, not little cones that you could run over. In some places vehicles were side by side, making it impossible to get around them. The most disturbing part was seeing dead bodies lying all over the place with flies starting to swarm around some of them. I saw a couple of crows on the chest of a dead woman near a crosswalk. They were proceeding to do nature's work and already feeding on her. It made me literally want to vomit, so I rolled down the window just in case.

Eventually I had to take the side streets all the way home because the main street was too blocked with dead bodies and vehicles. There were more people on the road now, like me, taking the side streets to wherever they were going. You could see it in their eyes that they were lost and confused. It felt like 9/11 again. The disbelief in their eyes and the look on their faces said, "I need to get home and see if this is real." I finally got home a half hour later, and that's when I knew it really was real. I could "feel" they were all gone as I stepped out of the truck. Oh, how alone I felt. Even though Lori was there, I still felt utterly and hopelessly alone.

Although I hadn't confirmed it yet, I knew my ten-year-old son Colin was gone too, and I started to cry again.

I walked up to the house, where Lori was on the front step. She had my Bible opened to a page toward the end of the book. She asked me, "What do you think happened?"

Lori was a lot of things, but two things she was not were naive or dumb. She knew what had happened. Otherwise my parallel bible (four bibles side by side in one bible) would not be at page 3160, Revelation 7. I said to her, "Lori, I'd wager that there are about 2.5 billion people who are dead right now, and another 2.5 billion wishing it was them instead."

# Chapter 11

# Left Behind

(Please note that pages 51 to 61 and pages 66 to 69 are purposely repeated from chapter 1 and 2 as to stay in the timeline)

I got up from the step after about ten minutes of talking to Lori about everything we had both experienced in the last hour. I slowly searched the house room by room, finding my family amongst the other dead guests in my house. In the living room I found my mother- and father-in-law as well as my mom. I didn't have to look long before I found my wife, Marie. She was in the kitchen facedown on the table with a cup of coffee close by. I didn't bother to lift her head; I didn't want to see the face of death again. Seeing Jeff dead and all those people dead on the street was enough for me. I chose to remember my wife the way she was as I kissed her lips and went off to work each morning.

It wasn't until I went upstairs that I found Stephan sitting cross-legged in Colin's room. I wondered why he was here; he should have been at school. It seems he was playing with YuGioh cards before he was taken. I knelt down and kissed the top of his head and gave him one last hug. As I stood up, I could feel a tear start to well up in my right eye and then one in my left, and then they wouldn't stop. I sat down beside him and wept like I did as a boy.

After a few minutes, I forced myself up and entered my bedroom. It used to be for just Marie and me, but now it held the remains of one of the other four couples who shared our room. *Well, that's two fewer people to share a room with,* I thought to myself. The other three couples would have already been at work when the rapture happened, so at least I wouldn't have to figure out what to do with their bodies. All I knew was that I had a total of sixteen dead bodies that I had to deal with. *Where are Sugar and Sydney anyway?* I wondered. I slowly made my way downstairs to the basement to find another couple of bodies. My dog Sugar was licking one of the bodies, and my cat Sydney was doing the same. They had belonged to neighbors of ours who lost their house to foreclosure because they couldn't afford the inflated price of food and still afford their home. I picked up the cat and walked upstairs and called for Sugar to "come." She wagged her stubby little border collie tail and ran up after me. I walked outside and sat on the front step and began petting the cat and the dog.

I'd always known about the rapture. I just always assumed I'd be taken; maybe that was my downfall. I had been so consumed by the story of Revelation and the awesome visual imagery that I got from it, that I had focused more on the story than on making sure I'd be ready for it. The rapture was what was supposed to happen after the 144,000 Jews were sealed. Many believed that the rapture would happen after twelve thousand Jews from each of the original twelve tribes were martyred or murdered.

I asked Lori to help me remove the dead bodies from the house starting with my mother- and father-in-law from the front living room, she nodded her head yes reluctantly. I put the cat down beside me on the step and got up and stretched a little. It wasn't going to be easy to get all those bodies out of the house. We started with my father-in-law, Peter. Lori grabbed her dad's feet and I grabbed his upper body under the arms like a fireman would do, and we dragged him out the front door.

Now the question was what to do with all the bodies. What were other people going to do with the bodies that they had in their houses? Lori and I brought Peter's body out to the front curb and proceeded to go get my mother-in-law Cindy's body. For now we would bring all the bodies to the curb and then figure out what to do with them. I had to place a sheet over Marie's body before we carried her out. I just couldn't bear to look at her. I felt as though I had let her down by not being with her. Although it was impossible, I imagined she was crying, looking down on me from heaven. We propped her up against the maple tree outside by the curb, and then I went to go get Stephan myself. As I passed the closet, I grabbed a few more sheets to cover all the bodies. I wrapped them all as best I could to help prevent animals or the flies from getting to them until I knew what to do.

By the time we got the now eighteen bodies out of the house, and all wrapped up, we were both exhausted. As I sat down again on the front step, I noticed a cop car down the street a bit, so I tried to flag him over. At first the officer just flashed his lights at me. After a couple of minutes, he finally pulled up and shut off the car, but he didn't bother to get out of his vehicle. It was hard to miss the pile of dead bodies, and I could tell he was deeply disturbed by the sight of them. He said, "One of your neighbours called and said they thought they had Charles Manson living down the street from them."

"Why's that?" I asked rhetorically.

He gestured with his hands spread to the bodies that lay to the left and to the right of him and asked, "What's this about?"

I replied, "The rapture happened. I had eighteen dead bodies in my house that were going to start smelling and decaying. I didn't know what else to do with them."

He scoffed and mocked me, repeating, "The rapture, hey? Turn on the radio and they'll tell you what to do with the bodies and what you should do over the next couple of days." Then he turned back on his car and slowly started to drive off.

I yelled out, "What station?"

He stopped the vehicle, poked his head out the window looking back, and said in a dull voice, "All of them."

# Chapter 12

# A New Leader

What could the radio tell me that I didn't already know? I flipped through the stations one by one, but they all seemed to be the same, just like the cop outside had said. The new US president, Victor Newton, was addressing the media at the temporary White House (since the real one had been destroyed in the great earthquake). I turned to the station with the best reception, which was 670 AM, and slowly increased the volume. I was sure I wasn't ready for what he was going to say. I had my own beliefs about what had just happened, and I highly doubted that he or anyone was going to tell everyone that the rapture had just happened. Even if he did, everyone would label him a fool and he would quickly be overthrown.

He began with "Ladies and gentlemen, we know the situation is the worst global attack known to mankind and that it has affected our brothers and sisters of every nation. We have reason to believe that an airborne virus has already overtaken millions upon millions of our citizens here in the United States, and our allies around the world tell us that the death toll is extremely high in their countries as well. Considering the numbers that are coming in, we believe the death toll to be in the billions worldwide. We have already held emergency meetings, and measures will be taken swiftly and decisively, with no mercy given to those involved in this horrific event.

"We vow to do our part. Now I implore you to do your part in this battle. It is imperative that we remove all the deceased bodies from every city and town to prevent the spread of disease. If you do not act quickly, many more will die from what you could have prevented. Every town or city council must organize all city and private trucks as well as gravel trucks and loaders to pick up all of today's deceased and bring them to one of the gathering points one mile outside of your city or town. You are to have a gathering place for these bodies at every provincial or state highway leaving your city or town. This is going to take all of us to do this, and therefore, beginning immediately, every town, city, and county is under marshal law.

"You have two hours to have all deceased bodies out of houses and such and onto the front boulevards. You have ten hours after that to get the deceased bodies to the gathering points. This is a very daunting task and cannot be done by the government alone. What this means is that anyone over the age of fourteen is hereby drafted and obligated to help remove the dead bodies and get them to the gathering points. Anyone who refuses will be put under arrest by an officer. Where an officer is not present, citizens are hereby authorized to put said person under a citizen's arrest and inform an officer as able. All those found guilty of noncompliance will be fined a minimum of ten thousand dollars to a maximum of a hundred percent of your annual income.

"Looting and riots will not be tolerated in the slightest, and all those suspected of such crimes will be shot on sight. These are very serious times and call for very serious actions. Today is the day that every citizen is needed to do the task at hand ... Please do not fail us and we will not fail you."

"What a load!" are the words that spilt from Lori's mouth.

"No doubt!" I said. "I don't trust that guy at all! He's only there because all his competition is dead. Anyone who could have beat him in the election died in the great earthquake."

I went up to my room and opened my Bible to Revelation. I thumbed through the pages past Revelation 7. I was pretty positive that all of that had already happened, considering half the world was dead. This is what I read.

> When he opened the seventh seal, there was silence in heaven for about half an hour. And I saw the seven angels who stand before God, and seven trumpets were given to them. Another angel, who had a golden censer, came and stood at the altar. He was given much incense to offer, with the prayers of all God's people, on the golden altar

in front of the throne. The smoke of the incense, together with the prayers of God's people, went up before God from the angel's hand. Then the angel took the censer, filled it with fire from the altar, and hurled it on the earth; and there came peals of thunder, rumblings, flashes of lightning and an earthquake. Then the seven angels who had the seven trumpets prepared to sound them. The first angel sounded his trumpet, and there came hail and fire mixed with blood, and it was hurled down on the earth. A third of the earth was burned up, a third of the trees were burned up, and all the green grass was burned up. (Revelation 8:1–7)

As I read these words, it was as if I had breathed life into them. The house began to shake violently. I cried out, "God, not again!" and hopped over the bed and started running down the stairs. As I hit the last stair on the landing, I stumbled and smashed into the wall with my right shoulder. I hit it with such a force that a bunch of drywall fell to the carpet in pieces when 210 pounds of weight came to a stop about six inches too late. "Eish" is all I said, but it rattled me enough to realize I had left my Bible upstairs. I ran back up the stairs and heard both upstairs windows explode from the violence of the earthquake. "What's going on? We don't have earthquakes in Winnipeg, God!" I grabbed the Bible and ran back down the stairs and heard Lori screaming for me to get out of the house. I raced for the front door and met Lori on the front boulevard and finally saw what she saw. The windows were all smashed, and the left lower wall started to buckle. Within the next thirty seconds, I watched on my knees as my house, which we had worked so hard to pay off, collapsed right in front of my eyes.

I looked on in shock, but there on my knees I saw God's awesome power raining down in the distance. I could hardly believe it: blood red hail the size of baseballs but even more unbelievable was the fire falling from the sky. It seemed to be in the distance, but as I looked straight up, I saw a ball of fire coming straight for my head. I rolled to the left, bumping into Lori and then using her as leverage to get up. I pulled on her hand and yelled, "Run!" I practically pulled her arm out of its socket as I dragged her to the fort in the backyard that I had built my two boys the previous

*Christ for Life*

year. It was small, but it was sturdy. It wasn't fireproof, but what was? We had to chance it.

Minutes seemed to pass, as we heard the pounding of the fiery hail all around us. After awhile we couldn't hear anything falling anymore, but man, could we feel the heat. Lori went to open the wooden door and flames engulfed her sweater and started her arm on fire. She pulled it back in and I had to pat out the fire on her arm. "Fudge nuts!" she screamed in pain. I couldn't help but laugh. The flames started to enter the fort so we had to climb out the window instead of going through the door. Easy enough, but Lori's not a small girl so it took a bit of work. I managed to just push her through the window. I didn't care; she could be mad at me later. As we stood on the gravel of the backyard, which also served as an extra parking space, it was just like I had read. Much of the grass and many of the trees and houses were now engulfed in flames. I was sure by the end of the day the whole city would be destroyed by fire. There was no way the fire departments could handle the magnitude of situation.

"Oh Lord, give me strength. I don't think I can handle this." I said.

That just changed everything! *We don't have time to wait around for a "death truck" to come pick up the bodies,* I thought to myself.

(Please note that pages 51 to 61 and pages 66 to 69 are purposely repeated from chapter 1 and 2 as to stay in the timeline)

I contemplated: now what were we supposed to do, and where were we supposed to go? I didn't know. All I knew was that I didn't want to be here when the scavengers came out. If history had taught me anything, it was that there will always be people who loot, steal, and kill for profit when a disaster happens. Just look at what happened when Hurricane Katrina hit New Orleans. I thought we better get started then and be one step ahead of them. I said to Lori, "Lori, go break in next door and get whatever food doesn't have to be refrigerated, and look for jewelry and money."

"Why?" is all she asked.

"Because we have no cash, and if we don't do it now, someone else will, and we will starve to death. Until the bullets start flying, I don't think anybody's going to listen now, considering all that's happened." That was good enough for her. She headed over to the house and reached her hand through the already busted front door window to unlock the door. After she went inside, I went to my backyard and opened the door to my garage, which was still for the most part standing strong for now after the earthquake and fires. I retrieved a box of firewood I had and a jerry can of gas I used for the lawn mower and snow blower through the years. I brought them out to the front street and stacked the whole box of firewood over my family's dead bodies. Then I poured most of the twenty litres of gasoline over the wood and the sheets covering the bodies. After that was done, I made a trail of gasoline to the other side of the street.

"Our father, who art in heaven, hallowed be thy name. Thy kingdom come, thy will be done, on earth as it is in heaven. Give us this day our daily bread; and forgive us our trespasses as we forgive those who trespass against us. And lead us not into temptation, but deliver us from evil. For thine is the kingdom, and the power, and the glory, forever and ever. Amen." After a long pause I lit the gasoline. As it raced toward the other side of the street, I said, "Please forgive me." At that moment, I heard a mighty *swoosh* as the fumes ignited and a tremendous ball of flames shot up from the pile.

I turned to Jeff's Hummer and unlocked the door. Lori came out with bags full of food and a baseball bat under one arm. She looked at the burning bodies, and then looked at me. She stopped for a second but then went to the truck, put the stuff in, and went to the next house. I went back to the other side of the street, and we continued to collect things from the houses we could until the truck was almost full. We drove to the end of our block and turned up Arlington, stopping at the Tesco station for gas, which luckily for us hadn't been hit by the hail fire. The pump wouldn't turn on, so I went inside, and that's when I noticed that the attendant was already dead on the floor. Not from the rapture—it seemed he had died from two shots in the chest. The killings had already started. I got behind the counter and hit the proper buttons to turn the pump on. Then I grabbed four jerry cans off the shelf and went outside to fill up the truck with gas and the jerry cans with diesel. I asked Lori to go in and get us something to eat and asked her to grab the microwave when she was finished. She came back out with a gun and some bullets she had found in the office as well as the bank deposit that the previous person had missed after shooting the attendant. I guess the other person was in too much of a hurry. Within five minutes we were back on the road and I was headed back to the shop where I worked. I guess now, its use to work because there was no way I was hanging around here anymore.

Although I was 99 percent certain that my son Colin had been taken, I was still drawn to go to his mom's house, just to check. I told Lori to guard the truck while I checked inside. The windows were all busted out from the earthquake, but I couldn't reach in through the window on the door without cutting my arm so I kicked the door open.

There were a few people dead here and there, but I didn't know any of them, so I carried on with my search. I honestly didn't expect to find Colin here anyway, so after I was finished, we drove over to my son's school. I wasn't going to find him alive there either, it seemed. I saw thirty or forty adults already outside, crying and hugging each other, but there didn't seem to be any children anywhere.

I assumed these people were parents just like me, but I didn't have time to stand around and cry right now. I quickly ran into the school and found my son's lifeless body bent over his desk. I had to yank on his body to get him loose of his desk, and then I carried him out to the vehicle. I had to put his body on top of the Hummer and strap it down, because there was no more room in the truck. I knew that the other parents were staring at me in disbelief, but I didn't have time to explain myself to these people. Now was the time to get out of Dodge, as the saying goes.

Everywhere we looked there was destruction and dead bodies. I just wanted to get back to the shop and switch everything into our newest work van, a two-year-old diesel Sprinter. It had a bunch of shelving in it, so it would be great for sorting everything later so we could easily find everything. Just as we turned onto Main Street from Leila, *SMASH!* "What the?" I shouted. Somebody had just rear-ended us, very hard. I started to slow down to see what was going on and it happened again. *SMASH!*

Lori screamed, "He's trying to run us off the road!"

My only thought was that he wanted our truck full of supplies, and with that thought, I swerved hard to the left and got in the other lane. I slammed on the brakes and yelled, *"Do something!"*

Without hesitation, Lori lifted the gun from under her leg. The man's vehicle came up quickly beside us, and she aimed squarely at her target and put a bullet in him. His car was still moving forward, but after hitting a parked car and then a tree, it finally came to a stop. The man still had his foot on the gas even though it was obvious he was dead. I put the truck in park, quickly rushed to his driver's-side door, pulled him out of the car, and turned it off. I looked in the backseat and found a full backpack, so I grabbed it. I took the keys out of the ignition and went back and opened the trunk. There was a large hockey bag and I tried to pull it out, but it was quite heavy and then it started to move! I dropped the backpack in surprise but then opened the zipper of the hockey bag. It moved again. I stepped back a bit. I'm telling you, I was freaked out! The bag continued to move and eventually opened more to expose a half-naked woman gagged and tied up. I'm not going to lie: she wasn't ugly. I didn't have a knife, so I opened the backpack and dumped it out onto the ground. Sure enough, I found a knife amongst the articles that a sick and twisted man would have to rape and torture his victim.

At this time Lori started coming out of the truck to see what was going on. I told the woman, "I'm not going to hurt you" as I put up my hands to symbolize my intentions. "I'm just going to cut the ropes off your wrists and then give the knife to you, okay?" She nodded yes, so I cut the ropes off the lady's wrists and handed her the knife. By now Lori was at the back of the car and looking at the contents of the backpack on the ground. She also saw the practically naked women getting out of the trunk.

I gave the woman my jacket and escorted her to the truck, passing on the other side of the vehicle so she didn't have to see what her fate would have been if this guy had had his way with her. Lori came and opened the back hatch of the Hummer and gave the lady a blanket, a pair of her jeans, and a sweater. The clothes were obviously too big, but she graciously accepted them saying, "Thank you. My name is Michelle." We all exchanged names, and Lori grabbed a jerry can and went back to deliver a final round of punishment to the man. She slowly poured some of the fuel onto the man and then the belongings of his backpack. She pulled out her lighter and lit the gasoline on fire. She only wished the man was still alive, for that was the punishment she felt he deserved.

As Lori came back to the truck, I realized we didn't have room for three people. I asked Michelle, "Do you want to come with us? Do you want us to leave you here, or do you want to be dropped off on the way out of town?"

"Where you going?" is all she asked.

"We don't know yet, other than far and north," I replied.

"North it is, then," she responded.

I asked Lori for the gun and climbed onto the roof of the truck, because there really wasn't enough room for three and we were only six blocks away from my work. I made sure that I was hanging on and that I was watching for another attack. I wouldn't let that happen again. We got to my workplace and transferred all the stuff into the Sprinter. When we were done I walked back into the shop and looked on the shelf where I had my invoices, lifted them up, and took the six hundred dollars from the cash sales I had down from my Thompson run. From there I went to the bathroom and rolled Jeff over to find his wallet. I opened the wallet to find another five hundred bucks and a few credit cards. I didn't think those would be any good anymore, but I took them just in case. "Sorry, Jeff," I whispered. I walked out of the bathroom, closed the door, and turned off the light. I locked up the shop and told Lori to take the Sprinter and drive up Highway 6 as far as we could possibly get away from anyone. I would drive the Hummer for now as protection.

Michelle asked if she could come with me, but Lori quickly said, "He just lost his wife and all his family. I think he needs some time to himself." She was right.

# Chapter 13

# Water

Well, just like the Bible says, no one will know the hour that one will be taken and one will be left behind, so it could be said that we didn't know how much time would pass before the next trumpet would blast. All we could know is that it would happen. The fifth, sixth, and seventh seals had all been opened in the last eight hours, along with the first trumpet blast, but who was to say when the next ones would come.

With that thought, I turned on the radio on the off chance that I might find something. *Tshhh, tshhh, tshhh* was all I could hear as I flipped from channel to channel, but in the end, two channels were working: 93.2 FM, the Christian radio station; and Hot 106.5 FM. Ironic, if you ask me. I turned it to the Christian station as I normally did, and it seemed I wasn't the only "Christian" who hadn't been taken. Chantelle Fisher was still there. That kind of threw me for a loop, because I'd listened to her for twenty years, and with her passion for God, I would have never guessed that she wouldn't be taken.

"I don't know about you," she said, "but I most definitely didn't prepare for this day. I didn't prepare to still be here, but I guess I didn't properly prepare to be taken, either. I sat here day after day and did my job, going through the motions, never realizing that that's all I was doing … going through the motions. What good is it to go to church, sit in the seat, sing a few songs, and hear the sermon if you never let it soak in? Never let it influence or change your life? Sure, it changed my life in the beginning, for the first few years, but then … here I am, so it's as plain as day that I missed the boat. But I won't miss the second boat, the second coming, and as God is my witness, I will witness to whoever is out there until that day!"

"Amen to that," I said out loud as I switched the station to Hot 106.5 to see what Adam Border had to say about what was going down.

"Eish, is all I can say! I don't know about you, man, but that was pretty intense! I thought I was going to die about ten times over! We've been scrambling to find out what exactly just happened, and everywhere we look, the answers are the same. Apparently there were large meteor showers, bigger than man has ever seen in any recorded history, and the United Nations voted on an aggressive tactic, as they felt that if the meteors were left to enter the Earth's atmosphere at their existing size, the world wouldn't survive. According to them, more than half the known nuclear weapons on the planet were used to try to protect us from annihilation.

"We asked a few local insurance companies about what happens now and found that the news isn't good. I don't know what the government is planning to do, but the insurance companies won't be paying a dime. They say this is an act of God—strike that—an act of nature, since who believes in God these days!" He chuckled slightly under his breath. "My advice to you is to take whatever is important to you and hide it! Hide it better than you've ever hidden anything, because the looters are already out and they're coming for it! I know we live in Canada so most of you probably don't have a gun, but let it be known that looters are allowed to be shot and killed on sight, so you might not want to stick around, because I predict it's going to get a little hairy around here for the next while!"

I turned back to 93.2 FM and thought, *that's why we're already gone.*

One of my favorite songs was playing; it's called "Mary, Did You Know." It's a phenomenal song about the magnitude of holding this little baby boy who would someday save all those who ask to be saved. Just imagine holding the future of the whole universe in your hands: would you even know that it was him? The next song that came on the radio was "Our God Is an Awesome God." That really tripped me out, because I had asked a teenager from our church at the time to play piano and sing both those songs at Marie's and my wedding. I felt drawn to pay deep attention. When the song was over, Chantelle Fisher started reading verses from the Bible. "We don't normally read Bible chapters or even that many Bible verses on this station, but as of right now, I'm the only one around here, so it's not like anyone is going to tell me I can't!" I laughed because she's not normally like that—she just does her job and doesn't ruffle any feathers. She started by reading the beginning of Revelation 1 and continued to chapter 8, verse 5, with a few comments of her own in between. Believe me, it was unheard of until then to hear so much Scripture read aloud on this radio station—or anywhere, for that matter.

She said, "Are you still listening? Are you really listening? If you are … then go get yourself some drinking water and read on … And then go get another glass. That's all I can tell you, man. The rest is up to you. If you won't seek the Lord at this hour, I won't give you the tools to take from my brothers and sisters in Christ. Find peace in the Lord and seek him out. Here's my favorite song of all time. I sang it two nights ago to my baby girl as she fell asleep." I could hear a faint cry as she started the song. She hadn't said it yet, but I assumed her daughter had been taken. The familiar tune that practically all Christians know came over the airwaves … "Amazing Grace."

I turned it up and sang along. At first I sang in a soft dull tone, but by the middle of it, I was singing at the top of my lungs, and I started to cry and weep for God's forgiveness and prayed for his guidance during this time. Lori and Michelle turned off the bypass and headed up Highway 6 to Thompson, but they pulled off on the shoulder, so I did the same and came to a stop.

I wiped my eyes before I walked up to the driver's-side window and Lori rolled it down. She said to me, "Do you have your Bible?"

"Yes," I replied.

"Go get it."

"Lori … really? Why right now?"

"Just go get it. I think it's really important."

"Fine!" I replied. I walked back to the Hummer, dug around a little, and brought it back, dropping it into her hands.

She gave it back to me and said, "You read it. Revelation chapter 8, verse 6 and on."

"You've been listening to the Christian radio station," I said.

"Just read it!" her voice demanded without sounding angry.

"Okay, okay," I said. So I started reading it.

"Out loud, you dough head!" she said, laughing.

I read aloud, "'Then the seven angels who had the seven trumpets prepared to sound them. The first angel sounded his trumpet, and there came hail and fire mixed with blood, and it was hurled down on the earth. A third of the earth was burned up, a third of the trees were burned up, and all the green grass was burned up.'"

Lori interrupted, "So that's where we're at right now. Now read the rest."

So I continued on. "'The second angel sounded his trumpet, and something like a huge mountain, all ablaze, was thrown into the sea. A third of the sea turned into blood, a third of the living creatures in the sea died, and a third of the ships were destroyed. The third angel sounded his trumpet, and a great star, blazing like a torch, fell from the sky on a third of the rivers and on the springs of water—the name of the star is Wormwood. A third of the waters turned bitter, and many people died from the waters that had become bitter.'"

"Above all other priorities, right now our top priority should be to obtain as much clean drinking water as humanly possible," Lori interrupted again. "I don't want to die from pure stupidity or necessity and drink contaminated water. We know it's coming. Better that we prepare than be stupid."

"Okay," I agreed. "There's a gas station just ten kilometers up the road. We'll buy everything they have." So that's what we did: we drove to the gas station. Lucky for us it was a fairly big gas station and it was open. We parked close to the entrance, and I walked in first. Lori and Michelle came in about a minute after me. I asked the woman at the counter if I could talk to the manager.

"That's me," she said.

"I want to buy all this water you have here on this pallet and those cases of pop next to it," I said. How much of a discount can I get if I buy it all? What will the total be?"

"You're serious? Why do you need that much? It would be way cheaper in town." She was more amazed than anything.

All I said was "I'm in a hurry and I don't really have time to go anywhere else." She started trying to figure it out slowly and it didn't seem like she was going to give me any kind of discount, so I quickly did the math for her on my phone. "You've got thirty cases of water there. The sign says $9.00 for a case. That's $270.00, and the pop is $2.99 each. Eight pops per case, that's roughly $24.00, times forty cases equals $960.00 plus the $270.00 for the water is $1,230.00 plus tax is $1377.60, so here's my credit card."

Immediately she said, "No way man— no credit cards here anymore after all the stuff that's gone on today. It's cash or nothing."

I opened my wallet again and said, "Fine—here it is" and quickly counted it out in front of her. I waited for her to hit the final button on the till, but instead she put the money straight into her pocket. *Somebody's working her own deal here, but why should I care?* I thought. I walked over to the cases of water and picked up three cases of twenty-four bottles. I carried them outside just as a couple was entering the store. I opened the back of the Hummer, and now I had to make a choice. I realized I didn't have enough room for all the water and the pop. I estimated I just barely had enough room for the water. I put the first three cases in and went back in to ask the girls for help and to talk about what we should do.

As I was walking back in, I saw the couple picking up cases of water that I'd already bought, so I said, "Hey, buddy, I already bought all that water and all that pop there. You have to get yours out of the fridge or from the back stockroom."

The girl from the counter said, "There is no more in the back, just what's in the fridge. How much do you want?"

The man said, "All of it! Plus what's in the fridge!"

The manager replied, "That'll be four thousand dollars."

The man said, "Sold" as he reached for his wallet.

I started walking to the counter and said, "I just paid you for all that water and pop" as I motioned to where the water and pop were.

She snorted back, "Where's your receipt?"

She could see the rage in my eyes. "You thief!" I exclaimed, and I started to come around the counter.

She raised a gun and said again, "Where's your receipt?" and this time she outright laughed. I stopped dead in my tracks, but the rage was so strong in me that I took another step forward, and she raised the gun to my head.

"His receipt is right here, lady!" I heard from behind me on my left. It was Lori's voice. As the girl behind the till glanced over to Lori, the gun followed her eyes and swayed away from my head. I lunged forward but heard *bang, bang*. I saw the reflections of the flash and heard another *bang*. Two to the chest, just like that, without even a hesitation. Lori was apparently a stone-cold killer who had been waiting all her life to be released! The manager had managed to fire off a shot, but luckily for us, Lori shot her while her gun wasn't focused on me and wasn't yet focused on Lori. The manager stumbled back against the wall and stood in disbelief for a moment. Then she slowly slid down the wall until she was hunched over on the floor.

"Don't even try it!" Lori sneered, and raised her gun to the couple as the man tried reaching into his jacket. He put his hand down, and Lori said, "Michelle, get his gun, and Declan, get the clerk's gun."

I grabbed the gun from the clerk, turned back to the couple, and raised my gun at them. Michelle walked over calmly, reached into the man's jacket, and took out a gun.

She opened it up and said, "It's not even loaded!"

The man said, "The bullets are in the car. I honestly didn't think I would need it yet."

Somehow that resonated with me, and I asked him, "What do you mean, not yet?"

He said, "You wouldn't understand. You're not a Christian."

Now it was my turn to laugh, and I did, out loud. Then Lori started laughing, and Michelle too. I said, "Funny thing is, sir, I am a Christian."

"Me too!" Lori and Michelle exclaimed.

"Thing is, in these crazy times where everything is changing so fast and greed is going to be rampant in many ways, we will do unto others before they do unto us. In other words, if we feel threatened in any way, we will do whatever it takes to survive, just as you've already seen Lori do."

I bent down again, dug into the clerk's pocket, pulled out my money, and then proceeded to check the rest of her pockets for cash. I found another $1,000 besides what was mine. As I stood back up, I asked the couple, "What's your plan?"

The woman was the first to speak. "You know, get some water, and get out of here as far as we can for now."

I said to her, "Okay, here's the deal … We don't have enough room for everything I bought anyways, and we don't have time to pick and choose what stuff to throw out instead of the water and pop, so like I said, here's the deal. You partner up with us and we'll take all the drinks from here and leave together. If we decide to split up later, we'll divide everything evenly and you can be on your way."

"Why should we trust you?" she asked.

"Because we have the guns, and if we wanted to, we could just kill you and take your vehicle and not have to worry about sharing," I said. "A person is only as good as their word, as the clerk found out, and I don't want to end up like her."

"Okay … My name is Sheila, and this is Lucas, my husband."

"My name is Declan, this is my sister-in-law Lori, and this is our new friend Michelle. Now that we've all been introduced, let's haul butt and get all these drinks in the vehicles before we have to shoot someone else who decides they want to try and take them from us."

We worked quickly, and within ten minutes the water and pop were completely gone from the store. We started on the food, but Sheila shouted, "Somebody's coming down the road in a car. We should leave!"

So we did. As much as you can haul butt loaded down with that much water, pop, and food, we got out of there and were on our way, farther down the road. I had no intention of driving up to Thompson. I just wanted to go somewhere far enough away from everyone so we could see someone coming from a mile away, and that place wasn't here.

We couldn't be sure how long it would be before the Wormwood star would fall and contaminate the water, or which water it would and wouldn't contaminate, but I guessed it would be sooner than later, based on the speed of events so far.

# Chapter 14

# Death will Elude Them

We drove a couple hundred kilometers north up Highway 6 until we saw what looked like cop cars up the road. At that point we turned off the main road, heading west. We drove toward Saskatchewan with no intentions of going that far, just trying to find a place far enough away that the average person wouldn't find us. A couple of hours farther down the road—a road I was sure no city folk had driven down in a long time—we found a small farm hidden by many trees, just the kind of place we were looking for. We searched around for a while but didn't find anyone. What we did find was a fair amount of dust, and that was fine by me, because it meant that no one had lived there for probably a couple of years. And with a little luck, maybe it'd be a couple more years before anyone pulled up into the driveway again. But just to be sure, we put our stuff away and hid the vehicles in the barn. We made sure to bring all our stuff upstairs; after all, out of sight, out of mind. After everything was put away I found a nice place under the shade of a large tree to bury Colin's body. I laid there crying beside his grave for over an hour, consumed with my guilt of how I had failed him.

Nobody knew how long it would take, but we kept tuned in to our friend Chantelle Fisher. Within a week we heard it on the radio: a star had fallen to the earth, contaminating much of the world's water.

> The second angel sounded his trumpet, and something like a huge mountain, all ablaze, was thrown into the sea. A third of the sea turned into blood, a third of the living creatures in the sea died, and a third of the ships were destroyed. The third angel sounded his trumpet, and a great star, blazing like a torch, fell from the sky on a third of the rivers and on the springs of water—the name of the star is Wormwood. A third of the waters turned bitter, and many people died from the waters that had become bitter. The fourth angel sounded his trumpet, and a third of the sun was struck, a third of the moon, and a third of the stars, so that a third of them turned dark. A third of the day was without light, and also a third of the night. (Revelation 8:8–12)

It seemed like God was letting us stay one step ahead of his plan. The question was why?

> "As I watched, I heard an eagle that was flying in midair call out in a loud voice: 'Woe! Woe! Woe to the inhabitants of the earth, because of the trumpet blasts about to be sounded by the other three angels!'" (Revelation 8:13)

Woe! Woe! Woe to the inhabitants of the earth! If that doesn't scare the tar out of you after all that has already happened! It's like God saying, *If you thought everything that's already happened was bad, you haven't seen anything yet. Expect it to be at least three times as bad! It's really going to suck living on the earth now!*

Every day that we listened to the radio, Chantelle told us that 1,000 people died here and 3,000 people died there. As the weeks went by, the numbers increased: 10,000 died here and 100,000 died there. Chantelle warned whoever was listening day after day that this was not the end, that man-attacking locusts would be coming just like it says in Revelation 9, and that we had best be prepared. How does one prepare for such a thing? Pray. Get down on your knees and pray.

*Christ for Life*

After about a month of hiding out on our small farm, we got the news from Chantelle that locusts had been attacking people in Iran. We decided to finally seek out a neighbor to see if we could find out more from the television. Until now we had had no intentions of ever seeking out anybody. We had to search a half dozen farms before we were finally greeted by a shotgun-toting ninety-year-old man, but he had cable, so we decided to chance it and tell him our story. He laughed a lot, but he finally let us in.

When we turned on the TV, what we saw were locusts exiting a deep shaft somewhere in Iran and attacking people. There seemed to be millions upon millions of the locusts, and every hour they were reported to have spread great distances. They were spreading out in all directions, and nothing seemed to be stopping them. Man, were they huge—the size of a large man's finger, with heads that look like a human's, and gnarly teeth. They looked like little horses with scorpion like tails and they seemed bent on torturing, not on killing. When they bit someone, the person would scream in pain and swat at the locust, but it seemed the more locusts a person killed, the more locusts would attack him or her. The locusts seemed to go for exposed skin first, so many people received nasty bites on their faces and arms, but if those were covered, the locusts still attacked by repeatedly stabbing their victim through their clothing with their scorpion like tails. Strangely, though, some people were unaffected by it. These people seemed to be different from the others. They would sit still as a swarm passed by, and from what we could see on the video, it seemed like they were praying.

For many days we traded stories with our newfound neighbour, John Wheatman. We found out that he had gone to church regularly until his wife passed away two years earlier. It was always her that wanted him to go, so he did, but now that she was gone, he didn't have much use for it.

As the days passed by, the swarms got closer to Canada. There were reports that they were riding the Gulf Stream across the oceans and would probably arrive within days. I didn't pray so much in my whole entire life as I did during this time. The locusts looked nasty enough on TV; I didn't need to experience firsthand what it felt like to get bitten by even one locust. After a couple of days, we seemed to be rubbing off on John, and he was praying too. Then I asked him where this church of his was and if he thought any of his neighbors were still around.

"Well, sure, Declan, it's just a few minutes up the way, and considering today is Sunday, I'm sure believers and nonbelievers alike will be there, seeing as how our locust friends are coming!" He laughed out loud and finished with a snort, which made me laugh as well, and then all the others joined in. I asked John if he thought the locals would mind if we showed up, and he said, "Sure they will, but it will be fun to get a rise out of them!" John was sure a funny guy for being ninety years old. That made me laugh. I sure appreciated him.

We arrived at church a little after nine, and although about twenty-five people were in the pews, there was no pastor. As we walked in, I whispered to John, "Where is the pastor?"

John replied, "He was taken along with his wife and kids the day of the rapture."

"So who does the teaching then?" I asked.

"Whoever gets the nerve first, I suppose …," John said.

With what felt like a nudging from God I opened my Bible to Revelation 9 and walked to the pulpit. "Good morning, friends. I'm here today with my friend John Wheatman and I wanna let you know about God's awesome power and his grace and mercy if we only accept it. First off, I'm sure you're all aware of God's awesome power lately and the example of it that's upon us now. I'm telling you, those locusts really freak me out! I've been praying since the day I saw them on the television that God would spare my friends and me from ever having to come face-to-face with one of those little buggers."

"But God has a different plan for us if we follow him. His plan is to see us walk through these times, not to merely survive them. With God on our side, we will walk out of this to the other side, preparing ourselves to walk alongside him. Please turn to Revelation chapter nine and follow along as I read."

> "'The fifth angel sounded his trumpet, and I saw a star that had fallen from the sky to the earth. The star was given the key to the shaft of the Abyss. When he opened the Abyss, smoke rose from it like the smoke from a gigantic

furnace. The sun and sky were darkened by the smoke from the Abyss. And out of the smoke locusts came down on the earth and were given power like that of scorpions of the earth. They were told not to harm the grass of the earth or any plant or tree, but only those people who did not have the seal of God on their foreheads. They were not allowed to kill them but only to torture them for five months. And the agony they suffered was like that of the sting of a scorpion when it strikes. During those days people will seek death but will not find it; they will long to die, but death will elude them. The locusts looked like horses prepared for battle. On their heads they wore something like crowns of gold, and their faces resembled human faces. Their hair was like women's hair, and their teeth were like lions' teeth. They had breastplates like breastplates of iron, and the sound of their wings was like the thundering of many horses and chariots rushing into battle. They had tails with stingers, like scorpions, and in their tails they had power to torment people for five months. They had as king over them the angel of the Abyss, whose name in Hebrew is Abaddon and in Greek is Apollyon (that is, Destroyer).' (Revelation 9:1–11)

"I repeat, 'During those days people will seek death but will not find it; they will long to die, but death will elude them.' Can this be any clearer? Those who are tormented will seek death but it will elude them. For five months! Not for five minutes or for five days, but for five months!"

"I lost my whole family in the last few months except for my sister-in-law Lori. I failed my family by not being ready when the rapture came, and I am choosing today not to fail the people who have been left behind. I will be ready and I want you to be ready too. If you have not already, please take the time to invite Jesus into your heart. Allow him to wipe your sin clean so you can be as white as snow. Never before in our lives until recently have we been able to so undeniably see that God is not happy with the world. So we must decide if we want to be a part of this world or be a part of God's world. If you truly love God, and you know he's there, pray to him and talk to him and trust in him like he is there. We have seen signs that believers have been spared from the torment of the locusts. Please be prepared with us, for it is my wish that none of you be lost. Amen."

"Let us sing a few songs, and maybe a few people could come and share their favorite verses that have gotten them through some tough times or helped them to be thankful for what they have. Afterward I invite you to John Wheatman's house and we can have a potluck of sorts. Let's start with 'How Great Thou Art.'"

The swarm took weeks to reach us here in Canada. People tried to do everything to stop the locusts, but those people got it ten times worse. We prayed every hour on the hour for God's grace in sparing us, and during the time of the swarm, we sought out our neighbors from whom we had wanted to stay far away at first. We wanted them to at least have the opportunity to seek God out so they could be saved before the swarm came. Many were saved by our personal testimonies and the realization that the swarm was coming, but many believed the swarm would never make it across the oceans or last through our cold winter, and they mocked us. But the locusts did come, and that winter the weather never got colder than 2°C. Those who mocked us ... well, needless to say, they weren't ready and paid dearly for it. Those of us who were saved weren't bitten even once, and we praised God that we were spared.

During the five months of the locusts, many Africans died from starvation while the rest of the world took care of themselves. Ironically enough, 100 percent of those that died of starvation had not even one bite from the locusts. However the 2 percent who were Africa's wealthy were very much alive and were so bitten and scarred that it was almost impossible to know who they were, or even if they were men or women.

The first woe is past; two other woes are yet to come. The sixth angel sounded his trumpet, and I heard a voice coming from the four horns of the golden altar that is before God. It said to the sixth angel who had the trumpet, "Release the four angels who are bound at the great river Euphrates." And the four angels who had been kept ready for this very hour and day and month and year were released to kill a third of mankind. The number of the mounted troops was twice ten thousand times ten thousand [200 million warriors]. I heard their number. The horses and riders I saw in my vision looked like this: Their breastplates were fiery red, dark blue, and yellow as sulfur. The heads of the horses resembled the heads of lions, and out of their mouths came fire, smoke and sulfur. A third of mankind was killed by the three plagues of fire, smoke and sulfur that came out of their mouths. The power of the horses was in their mouths and in their tails; for their tails were like snakes, having heads with which they inflict injury. (Revelation 9:12–19)

The only words to describe it would be *spontaneous combustion*. I saw people standing there and then all of a sudden they were running for their lives. The next thing I saw was them bursting into flames! Only the wicked seemed to be able to see their attackers coming, but in our minds' eyes, it was like we could see it all happening too. We were able to visualize it through the fear in their eyes as they ran this way and that. They died in a wave formation as the riders made their way from one wicked person to the next and consumed them by fire, smoke, and sulfur. It happened on February 5th, 2052, and was unlike anything I'd ever seen in my entire life.

"The rest of mankind who were not killed by these plagues still did not repent of the work of their hands; they did not stop worshiping demons, and idols of gold, silver, bronze, stone and wood—idols that cannot see or hear or walk. Nor did they repent of their murders, their magic arts, their sexual immorality or their thefts." (Revelation 9:20–21)

The wicked—I could hardly believe it was even possible, but they seemed to get more evil, and refused to listen to reason. Maybe if they had listened, we would have swayed some, but they would walk away from us and cover their ears, and many would spit upon us as we tried to witness to them. It infuriated them that their children would talk to us or even look at us, and many of them would scold and hit their children. But I could see it in the children's eyes: they were listening, they were being saved, and I could see a glow about them!

# Chapter 15

The Angel and the Little Scroll

Then I saw another mighty angel coming down from heaven. He was robed in a cloud, with a rainbow above his head; his face was like the sun, and his legs were like fiery pillars. He was holding a little scroll, which lay open in his hand. He planted his right foot on the sea and his left foot on the land, and he gave a loud shout like the roar of a lion. When he shouted, the voices of the seven thunders spoke. And when the seven thunders spoke, I was about to write; but I heard a voice from heaven say, "Seal up what the seven thunders have said and do not write it down."

Then the angel I had seen standing on the sea and on the land raised his right hand to heaven. And he swore by him who lives forever and ever, who created the heavens and all that is in them, the earth and all that is in it, and the sea and all that is in it, and said, "There will be no more delay! But in the days when the seventh angel is about to sound his trumpet, the mystery of God will be accomplished, just as he announced to his servants the prophets."

Then the voice that I had heard from heaven spoke to me once more: "Go, take the scroll that lies open in the hand of the angel who is standing on the sea and on the land."

So I went to the angel and asked him to give me the little scroll. He said to me, "Take it and eat it. It will turn your stomach sour, but 'in your mouth it will be as sweet as honey.' I took the little scroll from the angel's hand and ate it. It tasted as sweet as honey in my mouth, but when I had eaten it, my stomach turned sour. Then I was told, "You must prophesy again about many peoples, nations, languages and kings." (Revelation 10)

First society gave up on marriage, and then to add insult to injury, we gave up on God as well. The family broke down, and then society broke down. It became all about the individual's wants instead of the needs of society as a whole: "Forget everybody else; I am the most important person in my world." That's how it was back in 2010, and now, forty-some odd years later, I can't even begin to explain to you how bad it had gotten.

Sex sold everything. It sold cars, it sold movies, it sold shampoo, and it even sold food. Everywhere we looked, it was all about sex: where can I get it, who can I get it from, who else can I get it from, and what kind of nasty things can I get you to do for me? A long time ago, it stopped being about how can I find that one for me, and became how many can I find who will have sex with me.

On March 23, 2052, in the midst of all that had already happened, the seventh angel with the seventh trumpet came like a raging whirlwind and brought a sexually transmitted disease to rain fire on the wicked. It seemed to be saved for those who still, after all this, wouldn't repent, and they bathed themselves in their sexual immorality now more than ever. What a wicked disease this was. It was a combination of AIDS, leprosy, mad cow, herpes, and crabs. Someone couldn't have come up with a nastier, more resistant disease if they tried. Within sixty-six hours of contracting the sexually transmitted disease, patients would show very visible signs of cold sores on the face, leprosy in the hands, skin blotches from the AIDS virus, crabs, and shaking symptoms like mad cow to the point that they lost motor skills and the ability to control bodily functions. The patients all seemed to die within six days of their sexual encounter. Many people died very public, horrific deaths. It was impossible to hide that they had the disease.

We thanked God for the knowledge that was provided by the World Health Agency, which said that the few sexually monogamous, responsible couples they could find showed no signs of the disease. It seemed to affect only sexually promiscuous people. Many people did not want to believe this, but the math and the deaths spoke for themselves. Considering the short amount of time between infection and showing very visible signs of the disease, it was hard to believe that so many people got infected. It was a testament to how sexually promiscuous people really were that within a few months, millions were dying from the disease. The disease was nicknamed Sixty Six, because within sixty-six hours there were very visible signs that a person was infected, and within six days they were dead. Kids would tease other kids, saying, "You'd better stay away from so-and-so, or they'll Sixty Six your butt!"

# Chapter 16

# Two Witnesses

For more than two years our original five professed the Word of God to whoever would listen. We stayed out of the cities, but we walked from household to household, sharing the Word of God. When someone was receptive, we would stay the whole day and share with them the glory of God and how they could be saved from all that was yet to come in the coming days. Some followed along with us to learn more, and some to provide protection. We grew in size, and every time we got to twenty-four people in our group, we split and sent the other group in a new direction. We mapped out our courses so that we could be the most effective.

At the beginning, before we ever split into groups, we would often awake in the morning and share the dreams that we had had the previous night. They were eerily similar about events that would come to pass days later or sometimes weeks or months later. It seemed the more we prayed and professed about Jesus and God, the more God allowed us to see of his plan. We would often share these prophecies with the people to whom we were witnessing. Many came to the follow Jesus in this way, because it was so real to them.

By the spring of 2054, we had spread out so far that we had reached all of Canada, the United States, and even parts of Mexico. Granted, we didn't save as many people as we would have liked in the States, but we were able to save hundreds of thousands of people in Mexico. The poor are always much more willing to believe in something greater than themselves.

Lucas and I became tremendous friends over this time, and the ladies had bonded well too. As we often read Revelation from front to back, sometimes on a daily basis, we knew the things that were to come and we just knew the story was about to unfold in Israel. We were able to collect enough monetary donations to catch a freighter across the ocean. We didn't know how God was going to use us in Israel, but we felt him calling us there. On July 1, 2054, we had made our way to Washington, D.C. We planned to try to book a freighter to Israel, or to get as close as we could get and find our way from there. Two days before we were to leave, we found ourselves on a man's potato farm, witnessing to him and several other men.

The men attacked our group and immediately killed seven of the others who were with us. They beat Lucas and me, stripping us of all our clothing and stabbing each of us seven times. While we were at death's door, they forced us to watch as they raped and murdered Lori, Michelle, and Sheila. After they were finished, they shoved our faces in the puddles of blood, kicked us repeatedly, and then finally left us to die. Those men could have stabbed us seven times seventy and I believe that God would still have saved us. Because God still had a plan for us. We lay there naked and bleeding to death, writhing around in pain on the muddy ground for what seemed like hours. I don't know how it happened, but the more mud we got in our open wounds, the slower the bleeding became until finally it stopped.

The only thing for us to cover up with was empty potato sacks. We tore holes in one sack each and fashioned them into something resembling shorts, and fashioned others to look something like shirts. We walked barefoot through the field until we reached a house. To our horror, the men who had left us for dead were all on the front porch, drinking and laughing about what they had just done to "God's people," as they called us, and they mocked God. But as they saw us come up the driveway, they stopped talking and their jaws fell open in disbelief.

They didn't say a word, so I said to them, "As God is our witness for all the rest of our lives, we will profess God's great power over death to all we meet once we get to Israel. We will not change from the sack clothes as witnesses to what you wicked men did and tried to do. We will not be silenced until it is God's will that we be silenced, not yours!"

The men fled in all directions as they feared what God's wrath we might conjure up for them, and as they ran, I thought how fitting it would be if God smote (or struck down) each of the ten men the way he did to Lot's wife as he turned her into a pillar of salt. And as I thought it, it immediately happened! I looked at Lucas, stunned, and he looked at me in the same way.

We both said at the same time, "Did you see that! I thought it, and God made it immediately happen!"

"Whoa," I said. "You too?"

"Yes," he said. "I thought it and immediately it happened."

"We better be careful what we ask for!" I exclaimed.

"I guess so!" he said, half laughing. We found it quite hard to believe what had just happened and for quite a while, we examined the salt pillars the men had become. We prayed for our lost family and friends, and then we made our way toward the road.

We walked for hours along the road toward the freight yard, meeting no one along the way. It was fairly eerie to not come across anyone for so long. The crew of the ship showed great sympathy to us and sneaked us onto the ship without the captain knowing. For almost a week, the crew kept us hidden and we prayed for them all every day and evening and witnessed to them as well. We asked and prayed for a special blessing on them before they helped us sneak back off the boat in one of the tarp-covered loads they offloaded at the port. We finally reached Jerusalem on my birthday, July 18, 2054. Happy birthday to me! We had made it to the promised land!

That night in a vision, this is what God showed me.

The Two Witnesses

I was given a reed like a measuring rod and was told, "Go and measure the temple of God and the altar, with its worshipers. But exclude the outer court; do not measure it, because it has been given to the Gentiles. They will trample on the holy city for 42 months. And I will appoint my two witnesses, and they will prophesy for 1,260 days, clothed in sackcloth." They are "the two olive trees" and the two lampstands, and "they stand before the Lord of the earth." If anyone tries to harm them, fire comes from their mouths and devours their enemies. This is how anyone who wants to harm them must die. They have power to shut up the heavens so that it will not rain during the time they are prophesying; and they have power to turn the waters into blood and to strike the earth with every kind of plague as often as they want. Now when they have finished their testimony, the beast that comes up from the Abyss will attack them, and overpower and kill them. Their bodies will lie in the public square of the great city—which is figuratively called Sodom and Egypt—where also their Lord was crucified. For three and a half days some from every people, tribe, language and nation will gaze on their bodies and refuse them burial. The inhabitants of the earth will gloat over them and will celebrate by sending each other gifts, because these two prophets had tormented those who live on the earth.

But after the three and a half days the breath of life from God entered them, and they stood on their feet, and terror struck those who saw them. Then they heard a loud voice from heaven saying to them, "Come up here." And they went up to heaven in a cloud, while their enemies looked on.

At that very hour there was a severe earthquake and a tenth of the city collapsed. Seven thousand people were killed in the earthquake, and the survivors were terrified and gave glory to the God of heaven.

The second woe has passed; the third woe is coming soon.

## The Seventh Trumpet

The seventh angel sounded his trumpet, and there were loud voices in heaven, which said: "The kingdom of the world has become the kingdom of our Lord and of his Messiah, and he will reign for ever and ever."

> And the twenty-four elders, who were seated on their thrones before God, fell on their faces and worshiped God, saying: "We give thanks to you, Lord God Almighty, the One who is and who was, because you have taken your great power and have begun to reign. The nations were angry, and your wrath has come. The time has come for judging the dead, and for rewarding your servants the prophets and your people who revere your name, both great and small—and for destroying those who destroy the earth."
>
> Then God's temple in heaven was opened, and within his temple was seen the ark of his covenant. And there came flashes of lightning, rumblings, peals of thunder, an earthquake and a severe hailstorm. (Revelation 11:1–19)

As I woke in the morning, so did Lucas. I told him of my vision, and he ended and started my sentences, and I did his. It appeared we had had the same vision, and over the next 1,260 days just as God had said in the Bible and just as God showed us in our visions, all of it came to pass. What awesome power God gave us during this time. We had the benefit of knowing the exact day we would die, and we knew we had plenty of time to share our testimony and write it all down to share with others long after our deaths. Our only uncertainty was about who would finish the story, because it was far from over.

I ask you to remember this—if you remember nothing else, please remember this: God hates lukewarm people. In Revelation 4:15–16, God says, "I know you well ... you are neither hot nor cold; I wish you were one or the other! But since you are merely lukewarm, I will spit you out of my mouth!"

In life we must all pick a side. Some choose to sit on the sidelines of life or sit down right in the middle of the field and say, "I'm not on your side and I'm not on your side." How angry would you be if you were playing a soccer or football game and six people decided they were going to sit around in the middle of the field, picking dandelions and pulling blades of grass. But your opponent was wise, and scored on you by using these six "basically good people" as shields so he could score on you. Would you care that they were basically good people then?

Now imagine that there is a war going on and those same six people are standing around on the frontline of a battle between you and your enemy. Your enemy is using these six "basically good people who don't want to get involved" as shields to hide behind, and he's killing your men. How long will it take before you kill these six basically useless people who are getting your men killed as they stand in your way? I ask again, how long?

# Chapter 17

Revelation 12

A great sign appeared in heaven: a woman clothed with the sun, with the moon under her feet and a crown of twelve stars on her head. She was pregnant and cried out in pain as she was about to give birth. Then another sign appeared in heaven: an enormous red dragon with seven heads and ten horns and seven crowns on its heads. Its tail swept a third of the stars out of the sky and flung them to the earth. The dragon stood in front of the woman who was about to give birth, so that it might devour her child the moment he was born. She gave birth to a son, a male child, who "will rule all the nations with an iron scepter." And her child was snatched up to God and to his throne. The woman fled into the wilderness to a place prepared for her by God, where she might be taken care of for 1,260 days.

Then war broke out in heaven. Michael and his angels fought against the dragon, and the dragon and his angels fought back. But he was not strong enough, and they lost their place in heaven. The great dragon was hurled down—that ancient serpent called the Devil, or Satan, who leads the whole world astray. He was hurled to the earth, and his angels with him.

Then I heard a loud voice in heaven say: "Now have come the salvation and the power and the kingdom of our God, and the authority of his Messiah. For the accuser of our brothers and sisters, who accuses them before our God day and night, has been hurled down. They triumphed over him by the blood of the Lamb and by the word of their testimony; they did not love their lives so much as to shrink from death. Therefore rejoice, you heavens and you who dwell in them! But woe to the earth and the sea, because the Devil has gone down to you! He is filled with fury, because he knows that his time is short."

When the dragon saw that he had been hurled to the earth, he pursued the woman who had given birth to the male child. The woman was given the two wings of a great eagle, so that she might fly to the place prepared for her in the wilderness, where she would be taken care of for a time, times and half a time, out of the serpent's reach. Then from his mouth the serpent spewed water like a river, to overtake the woman and sweep her away with the torrent. But the earth helped the woman by opening its mouth and swallowing the river that the dragon had spewed out of his mouth. Then the dragon was enraged at the woman and went off to wage war against the rest of her offspring—those who keep God's commands and hold fast their testimony about Jesus. (Revelation 12:1–17)

The Beast Out of the Sea

The dragon stood on the shore of the sea. And I saw a beast coming out of the sea. It had ten horns and seven heads, with ten crowns on its horns, and on each head a blasphemous name. The beast I saw resembled a leopard, but had feet like those of a bear and a mouth like that of a lion. The dragon gave the beast his power and his throne and great authority. One of the heads of the beast seemed to have had a fatal wound, but the fatal wound had been healed. The whole world was filled with wonder and followed the beast. People worshiped the dragon because he had given authority to the beast, and they also worshiped the beast and asked, "Who is like the beast? Who can wage war against it?"

The beast was given a mouth to utter proud words and blasphemies and to exercise its authority for forty-two months. It opened its mouth to blaspheme God, and to slander his name and his dwelling place and those who live in heaven. It was given power to wage war against God's holy people and to conquer them. And it was given authority over every tribe, people, language and nation. All inhabitants of the earth will worship the beast—all whose names have not been written in the Lamb's book of life, the Lamb who was slain from the creation of the world.

Whoever has ears, let them hear.

"If anyone is to go into captivity, into captivity they will go. If anyone is to be killed with the sword, with the sword they will be killed."

This calls for patient endurance and faithfulness on the part of God's people.

The Beast Out of the Earth

Then I saw a second beast, coming out of the earth. It had two horns like a lamb, but it spoke like a dragon. It exercised all the authority of the first beast on its behalf, and made the earth and its inhabitants worship the first beast, whose fatal wound had been healed. And it performed great signs, even causing fire to come down from heaven to the earth in full view of the people. Because of the signs it was given power to perform on behalf of the first beast, it deceived the inhabitants of the earth. It ordered them to set up an image in honor of the beast who was wounded by the sword and yet lived. The second beast was given power to give breath to the image of the first beast, so that the image could speak and cause all who refused to worship the image to be killed. It also forced all people, great and small, rich and poor, free and slave, to receive a mark on their right hands or on their foreheads, so that they could not buy or sell unless they had the mark, which is the name of the beast or the number of its name.

This calls for wisdom. Let the person who has insight calculate the number of the beast, for it is the number of a man. That number is 666. (Revelation 13)

# Chapter 18

# Victor

Let's just say I found this journal the other day and it intrigued me enough that I thought I would continue on with the story through another set of eyes. This is my first entry into this journal, so I will introduce myself. My name is Victor Newton; I am the grandson of Frank Newton, who was the inventor of the biochip, or microchip. After my grandfather died, it was my father's work that saw the Natas chip installed in every known criminal in China in 2038 while he kept our family in Washington, D.C.

Great peace had come to China during this time, but not for our family. On December 25, 2038, as our family gathered outside our home, my sister and I were already waiting in the car, ready to go visit relatives. It was then that a man walked right up to my father and mother and murdered them in the driveway, right in front of our eyes. I pushed my sister Natasha out of the other side of the car, and as I was exiting, I heard a shot ring out. I fell to the ground, and then I heard six more shots ring out. I later found out that my father's chauffeur, John Videl, shot the assailant six times in the back as he was climbing through the backseat of our car to come finish me off. The attacker was a follower of a popular TV evangelist named Henry White, who pumped propaganda that the Natas chip was the Devil's tool to enslave us all.

My sister ended up in a psychiatric ward for just under a year after multiple suicide attempts before she finally got it right one night and slit her neck instead of her wrists on the anniversary of our parents' death. I, on the other hand, ended up in a wheelchair paralyzed from the neck down. I couldn't have committed suicide even if I'd wanted to.

After my sister's death, I tried to sue Henry White for his hand in creating the monster that killed my whole family, but White was a rich man by this time, selling salvation to any poor sap who had a credit card. So instead I spent all my energy on spreading the use of the Natas chip throughout the world to monitor criminals and civilians alike. After all, not all criminals are known to the police; some are criminals for decades before they ever get caught for a crime. After I'm finished with them, they won't be able to urinate without the World Natas Security System (WNSS) knowing which stall they're in and whether they are sitting down or standing up peeing on the seat!

For three long years, we ran commercials telling civilians all the benefits and freedom that citizens could have with the Natas chip: security, safety, health records—all the positive spin I could put on it. By 2048, we had reached a million US citizens who were willing to have the chip inserted of their own free will. I lobbied the American government to adapt my policies and to embrace the possibilities of the Natas chip, but every time it made it through Congress, the president would veto the policy. Lucky for us the president and vice president had both been killed in the great earthquake on July 18, 2051. Because many of the Cabinet and Senate seats were empty as well, I used all the money I had at my disposal to run for office, and by a landslide 70 percent, I was elected president of the United States. How could anyone not vote for me? I was the poster child of justice, if you ask me. If you wanted justice, I was your man, and 70 percent of the voters agreed!

Because of the turmoil the continent was in—never mind the country—I as well as my colleagues pressed Canada and Mexico for martial law to be imposed indefinitely. It was headed by the United States, and for once we were seen as a great continent instead of just a country, rising out of the ashes. I pushed for uniformity throughout all provinces, states, cities, and towns so that everyone knew what was happening at all levels of government. Every cent was accounted for, the big bonuses, expense accounts, and huge salaries became a thing of the past, and I experienced the highest approval rating of any president. Ours was the first continent to become a great nation. Congress passed a law requiring the Natas chip to be implanted in all citizens, and the program was set to start on December 31, 2057.

For the next three and a half years, I built our continent to be a superpower among the seven continents and encouraged the other continents to embrace the value of this new political system. We called ourselves the C7. In this system no one was left out: there were no trade embargos, no favorites, and we even started a global defense team made up of a million troops. Each continent paid for a minimum of 14.3 percent of the cost to equip and ship them anywhere they were needed in the world. The first place all million troops were sent to was Africa. They moved from town to town, killing all resisters to peace to restore order to places like the Congo that hadn't seen order for decades. Many people died in those first six months, but after a while, the resisters stopped resisting as they knew they were grossly outnumbered. The C7 vowed that if order was not restored, a draft would happen worldwide to increase the troops to 2 million. In December 2057, the last known resistance to order was scheduled to be crushed in Israel four days before the implementation of the Natas chip worldwide. The C7 through minimal persuasion chose to follow our lead and start the implementation of the Natas chip throughout the C7.

2058 was going to be our year—my year. Everyone in the world would know my name by the time the year was over. Like it or not, no one would be allowed to travel from town to town, let alone from country to country, without having a Natas chip. Nor would they be allowed to buy or sell anything unless it was tracked through their Natas chip. By the time I was finished, they wouldn't be able to breathe without it.

As most people know, religion was pretty much wiped out after the great earthquake of 2051. But since then, many people had been following two prophets named Lucas and Declan around the continent and then in Israel. These two had been thorns in my side for the past three and a half years. That's all I needed: fanatical Christians to deal with. They both had aggravated me for a long time. The last resisters, as luck would have it, were the prophets Lucas and Declan and their followers. I called upon my good friend Dr. Juliard, who had studied all faiths for the last forty years, to advise me in how to proceed with these two resisters. Dr. Juliard was a world-renowned psychic who had helped many through his television broadcasts to millions if not billions of people. He had helped solve many murder cases and advised political leaders such as myself for many years.

He seemed to possess power and knowledge beyond anyone else's and was said to have healed people from great sicknesses, even bringing some back from the dead. He was the guy I needed since these two prophets were different from any other people the global defense team had come upon before. These two prophets seemed to have magical powers and were able to summon locusts, fire, or whatever else they wanted against their enemies. We lost 100 men in one day fighting against these two men as they spit fire out of their mouths to consume their enemies.

Many said that they had the power of God behind them, but with the help of Dr. Juliard, we would use the power of the media to show the nations that these were just magic tricks and superstitious testimonies of simple-minded people who shouldn't be trusted. Dr. Juliard vowed that he would upstage these two imposters and that we would be finished with them. That was something I was looking forward to.

As a show of good faith, Dr. Juliard and I called a press conference in a Jerusalem courtyard to talk with the prophets Lucas and Declan on the evening of December 27, 2057. We wanted to use this as a platform to present to the world the benefits of the Natas chip. As we all gathered, it quickly became a war of words. It escalated into shouting back and forth about God and the downfalls of religion until I yelled, "There is no God, so why are you twisting the minds of all your followers to believe that the Natas chip is the Devil's tool? If there is no God, then it stands to reason that there is no Devil!"

"Blaspheme, lies spill from your lips Victor for the last time!" Declan exclaimed.

I saw prophet Declan's wooden staff rise into the air and transform into a steel sword right before my eyes. It came down swiftly, and at first I thought it missed me, but then I felt warm blood flow from my neck like a river as it soaked my white shirt. I felt my head tilt back, and my eyes followed until I saw Dr. Juliard behind me. I seemed to sway to the left, and then I dropped to my knees out of my wheelchair and blacked out. I cannot give a personal account of the rest; all I know is what people who were there told me and what I saw on the video.

Dr. Juliard started to chant, "Spirits rise up and destroy these two men!" Again and again he said this: "Spirits rise up and destroy these two men." After the third chant, the first prophet was attacked from behind and then the other. A book dropped out of the sackcloth Declan was wearing and fell to the ground. Dr. Juliard quickly picked it up while the two men dressed in sackcloth were repeatedly attacked by a seemingly invisible assailant if not by multiple assailants. You could not see them, but you could see the wrath of their fury on these two self-professed prophets of God.

The attack was long and drawn out made to make them suffer and to make an example of them. It was apparent to anyone that these two men didn't stand a chance against their attacker. After what seemed like a minute had passed, Dr. Juliard started chanting, "Finish them," and they were thrown into the air. As they fell back down, two, four-foot-long spikes appeared and impaled each man in the back, and they both screamed in pain as they died. Then Dr. Juliard picked up the sword and beheaded both the prophets and threw the sword back onto the ground. As he did this, the sword turned back into a staff.

The crowd cheered and praised the spirits for killing these two men, and they also praised Dr. Juliard, for these two prophets had brought the citizens much grief over the last three and a half years, and they were happy to be rid of them.

Dr. Juliard said, "Do you want to see the true power of the spirits that I alone yield with my master's permission?"

"Yes!" the crowd yelled. "Yes!"

"Master, heal President Victor Newton, for your servant has asked you to show your power over death, and to show that you are superior to the God whom the prophets Lucas and Declan served." Dr. Juliard slid his hand under my neck and raised his forearm to raise my head as to close the gap that practically severed my head from my neck. The wound spread seven inches from ear to ear. He then placed his other hand over the entire wound and praised, "Master, heal him, Master, heal him, Master, heal him so the whole world will know that it is your time to rule this earth!"

When I woke up in Dr. Juliard's arms, I was lying in a pool of my own blood. It looked like a murder scene; I don't know how I even survived. People tell me I have Dr. Juliard and the Master to thank for that. I could still feel the excruciating pain of having my head practically cut off, but for all intents and purposes, I was healed. Many people were screaming in disbelief or in awe; some even fainted. Dr. Juliard helped me to my feet and told me to walk. It was a miracle! For the first time since I had been shot nineteen years earlier, I was able to walk again!

Dr. Juliard declared, "We will rejoice in our enemies' defeat and the awesome power of the Master for healing my good friend and fellow follower Victor Newton. Our Master is so great, he even healed Victor's paralyzed body and has made him able to walk again!"

As we left, Dr. Juliard handed me a book and told me it was the prophet Declan's. He laughed and said Declan obviously didn't need it anymore so I might as well check it out. As we left the area, I ordered extra security for the courtyard, for in three and a half days, we would launch the worldwide implementation of the Natas chip. For the next three and a half days, the people celebrated, partied, and even exchanged gifts to commemorate the falling of the prophets and the rising of President Victor Newton. They refused to bury the two prophets, mocking them and even spitting on their bodies.

# Chapter 19

# Rise Up

Three days later, here we were again, but this time I was greeted like a rock star! I walked around the stage as people cheered. The people said, "Who is like President Victor, who was mortally wounded but was brought back from the dead? What man is greater than he?"

Dr. Juliard answered, "No man is greater than President Victor, for he will lead us into a new world with new beginnings!"

All the people cheered and shouted, "Praise be to Victor, praise be to Victor, and praise be to Dr. Juliard, praise be to Dr. Juliard!"

But as they did this, a spirit of life entered the bodies of the two prophets who had been dead for three and a half days. Their severed heads were once again part of their bodies but you could see the scars from where the sword had cut off their heads. As they stood up, a loud voice that came unmistakably from the sky called out to these two prophets, saying, "Come up!"

And then at that command, the two rose into the cloudless sky in front of all their enemies. They rose for two minutes until they could be seen no longer, and then a great earthquake followed, destroying a tenth of the great city and killing 7,000 of the people celebrating in the courtyard.

The people screamed in terror, "Please God, please God, father of Jesus, please forgive us!"

But was it too late for them? Were they calling out because they truly wanted to follow God, or were they calling out to whomever they thought might save them?

# Chapter 20

# Christ for Life

My good friend Dr. Juliard proved to be a very useful ally; he even got one of his friends to make a larger-than-life-size statue of me and erected it on the very spot where the two prophets were finally crushed. We were to have a grand unveiling of the statue before I announced the mandatory implantation of the Natas chip. The implementation was postponed six months so we would have time to clean up the city, since the earthquake had nearly destroyed it.

I thought I would tell them a good joke about my death. People seemed to laugh a kind of soft, eerie laugh when I joked with them about my death. It acted as a good reminder that people should be well aware of Dr. Juliard and me, because we had powers on our side that they had never seen before.

As the statue was unveiled, Dr. Juliard shouted, "Who is like our leader, Victor?"

"No one!" three men close to the middle of the crowd shouted.

Again Dr. Juliard shouted, "Who is like our leader, Victor?"

Once again the three men shouted, "No one!" But this time more of the crowd joined in shouting, "No one."

A third time Dr. Juliard shouted, "Who is like our leader, Victor, for he was victorious over his enemies and over death?"

"No one!" the whole crowd shouted. I swear Dr. Juliard paid those three men to be there! That made me laugh inside.

But one brave young man cried out, "My God and his son, Jesus, are greater than any man or any other God!"

Dr. Juliard looked at this man with rage in his eyes but calmly said, "You may want to think so, but this is Victor's time, and all will bow, and all will receive the mark of the Natas 666 chip. All those who don't will not be able to buy or sell any goods from this day forward without it."

The man cried out again, "I will never take the mark of the Devil!"

"Foolish man, because of your arrogance, you will be the first on this day! Guards! Arrest this man and strap him to the chair!" As they grabbed the man by his shirt, he wriggled free of his shirt and their grip. This exposed a full cross on his back with three large letters on the top of the cross—C.F.L.—and on a banner wrapped around the cross it read "Christ for Life." The man took a few steps back, but this time they got a better hold of him, and Dr. Juliard changed his mind and ordered the men to tie him to a tree. As they did this, he ordered another guard to go get a whip.

When Dr. Juliard was handed the whip, he pulled a knife out of his pocket, cut open the end of the whip, unraveled it about ten inches to expose multiple individual threads, and tied it off again so that it would not unravel further. He calmly put his knife back in his pocket and said, "All those who resist will be treated as enemies of the C7 and enemies of the peace that the Natas chip will bring, and all will be dealt with accordingly." He whipped the man and with each lash of the whip he bled more and the cuts went deeper. After the fifth time, the man screamed in pain, but Dr. Juliard did not stop. Instead he simply said, "Receive the mark or die as a resister to peace."

"Have mercy on him!" a woman cried.

"There will be no mercy for those who resist the new way, for those who resist peace," Dr. Juliard said calmly.

"I will receive the mark, but please just stop whipping him!" she cried.

"His life will be spared today, but for as long as he does not take the mark, we will not bandage his wounds, and he will surely die from infection in a few days. All who resist will be dealt with harshly, and from this man forward, I guarantee you it will be a painful, public death." Dr. Juliard picked up a sword and walked toward the beaten man. As he drew nearer, he raised the blade over his head, poised to strike to demonstrate his power over the man.

"Please, God, take me now!" the man cried. Just then, Dr. Juliard tripped, bringing the sword upon the man's neck and cutting his head clear off.

The woman screamed, but Dr. Juliard pointed the sword at her, and she quickly stopped. "Get in the chair," he said to her. "Guards, put the mark on the foreheads of those who resist even in the slightest, so we will forever know who resisted peace. All the others will receive the mark on their right hand. All will bow down to the Master; all will bow down to Victor Newton, whom our Master has chosen to lead us through these trying times. All who resist as this man has, will be executed in the same way."

The guards blocked the exits of the courtyard, and no one else bothered to resist. After all, most of the people who were in the courtyard were here to see Dr. Juliard and me speak. They may have had second thoughts after what they had just seen, but most of them were obviously supporters or too cowardly to resist, because they had just witnessed the execution of the one man who did try to resist.

As much as we were in control, we were also not in control. Pockets of resistance kept popping up here and there all over the world, protesting the Natas chip. Many of the resisters had a crest or a tattoo saying "C.F.L." and then "Christ for Life" written underneath. This infuriated me, but how could you make an example of people who were willing to die for what they believed in? At first we made their beheadings public, but this only seemed to make the Christ for Life movement spread like a wildfire. So eventually we chose to beat the fire down as quietly as we could.

# Chapter 21

### The Lamb and the 144,000

Then I looked, and there before me was the Lamb, standing on Mount Zion, and with him 144,000 who had his name and his Father's name written on their foreheads. And I heard a sound from heaven like the roar of rushing waters and like a loud peal of thunder. The sound I heard was like that of harpists playing their harps. And they sang a new song before the throne and before the four living creatures and the elders. No one could learn the song except the 144,000 who had been redeemed from the earth. These are those who did not defile themselves with women, for they remained virgins. They follow the Lamb wherever he goes. They were purchased from among mankind and offered as firstfruits to God and the Lamb. No lie was found in their mouths; they are blameless.

### The Three Angels

Then I saw another angel flying in midair, and he had the eternal gospel to proclaim to those who live on the earth—to every nation, tribe, language and people. He said in a loud voice, "Fear God and give him glory, because the hour of his judgment has come. Worship him who made the heavens, the earth, the sea and the springs of water."

A second angel followed and said, "Fallen! Fallen is Babylon the Great," which made all the nations drink the maddening wine of her adulteries.

A third angel followed them and said in a loud voice: "If anyone worships the beast and its image and receives its mark on their forehead or on their hand, they, too, will drink the wine of God's fury, which has been poured full strength into the cup of his wrath. They will be tormented with burning sulfur in the presence of the holy angels and of the Lamb. And the smoke of their torment will rise for ever and ever. There will be no rest day or night for those who worship the beast and its image, or for anyone who receives the mark of its name." This calls for patient endurance on the part of the people of God who keep his commands and remain faithful to Jesus.

Then I heard a voice from heaven say, "Write this: Blessed are the dead who die in the Lord from now on."

"Yes," says the Spirit, "they will rest from their labor, for their deeds will follow them."

Harvesting the Earth and Trampling the Winepress

I looked, and there before me was a white cloud, and seated on the cloud was one like a son of man with a crown of gold on his head and a sharp sickle in his hand. Then another angel came out of the temple and called in a loud voice to him who was sitting on the cloud, "Take your sickle and reap, because the time to reap has come, for the harvest of the earth is ripe." So he who was seated on the cloud swung his sickle over the earth, and the earth was harvested.

Another angel came out of the temple in heaven, and he too had a sharp sickle. Still another angel, who had charge of the fire, came from the altar and called in a loud voice to him who had the sharp sickle, "Take your sharp sickle and gather the clusters of grapes from the earth's vine, because its grapes are ripe." The angel swung his sickle on the earth, gathered its grapes and threw them into the great winepress of God's wrath. They were trampled in the winepress outside the city, and blood flowed out of the press, rising as high as the horses' bridles for a distance of 1,600 stadia [183.93 miles]. (Revelation 14)

## Seven Angels with Seven Plagues

I saw in heaven another great and marvelous sign: seven angels with the seven last plagues—last, because with them God's wrath is completed. And I saw what looked like a sea of glass glowing with fire and, standing beside the sea, those who had been victorious over the beast and its image and over the number of its name. They held harps given them by God and sang the song of God's servant Moses and of the Lamb: "Great and marvelous are your deeds, Lord God Almighty. Just and true are your ways, King of the nations. Who will not fear you, Lord, and bring glory to your name? For you alone are holy. All nations will come and worship before you, for your righteous acts have been revealed."

After this I looked, and I saw in heaven the temple—that is, the tabernacle of the covenant law—and it was opened. Out of the temple came the seven angels with the seven plagues. They were dressed in clean, shining linen and wore golden sashes around their chests. Then one of the four living creatures gave to the seven angels seven golden bowls filled with the wrath of God, who lives for ever and ever. And the temple was filled with smoke from the glory of God and from his power, and no one could enter the temple until the seven plagues of the seven angels were completed. (Revelation 15)

CHAPTER 22

# The Mark

"The Seven Bowls of God's Wrath

Then I heard a loud voice from the temple saying to the seven angels, 'Go, pour out the seven bowls of God's wrath on the earth.' The first angel went and poured out his bowl on the land, and ugly, festering sores broke out on the people who had the mark of the beast and worshiped its image." (Revelation 16:1–2)

Two and a half years had passed since the Natas chip had been implemented worldwide. Great amounts of prosperity had been shared between the leaders of the C7. I never thought it was possible for me to obtain that much wealth. I never thought I'd see the amount of money one company would pay me just to hold off a month or even a few days before allowing a competitor to process Natas chip transactions. A million dollars here, ten million dollars there, just to slow down another company from having access to a chip that I, Victor Newton, already controlled! It was beautiful! *So how is this possible?* I asked myself today after I woke up and looked in the mirror. *How is it possible when both the prophets are dead that I could wake up looking like this? Only God himself could make this happen; otherwise, how did I get these ugly, disgusting sores on my body? I'm Victor*

*Newton, leader of the whole free world! How does this happen to me? How am I supposed to spin this so all those Bible thumpers don't think they've gotten the better of me? I better call Dr. Juliard. Maybe he'll know what to do.*

I checked the news as I waited for Dr. Juliard, and found out that I was not alone in this sudden disfigurement. Even though the newscaster tried to cover it with makeup, it was obvious that he had sores just like mine. He was interviewing top doctors from around the world. Everyone had a theory and they all had the disfigurement, but not one of them had a clue where it came from, or so they said.

Hours later, Dr. Juliard arrived and half laughed at me, which only infuriated me more! "Relax, I'll take care of it. All you have to do is say what I say," he said. "Repeat after me: Master, please hide what my enemy has done to me so that no man may see. Master, please hide what my enemy has done to me so that no man may see. Master, please hide what my enemy has done to me so that no man may see." We said it together.

"Now, go look in the mirror," Dr. Juliard said.

"It's gone," I said in disbelief. "It's really gone, but why does it still hurt?"

"Well." Dr. Juliard paused. "It's not really gone … It's more like … hidden."

"What do you mean, hidden?" I asked.

"What God has done, no one can undo, not even the Master," he said.

"Look! You said we were on the winning side of this whole God versus the Devil battle. You said that we were going to come out on top!"

"We will, Victor, but what, you didn't think there'd be a few hiccups along the way? You thought God would just roll over and play dead?" Dr. Juliard asked sarcastically.

"Yes! That's exactly what I thought he would do! That's exactly what he's been doing my whole life! Where was he when my parents were murdered? Where was he when I got shot in the back and was paralyzed? Where was he then? I couldn't give a hoot about God and what his plans are! My only plan is to mess up his plans and get rich doing it! Forget God and whatever his plan is!"

"You already know why your parents were murdered, and why that man tried to murder you. There are three types of people in this world, Victor: those who try to help God's plan, those whom the Master uses for his plan, and the other useless pawns each side uses to get in the way of the others' plans. Your attacker thought he was helping God when he killed your parents. He was trying to stop the spread of the Natas chip. When he saw you there, he realized he had to kill you too if that was to be possible. Lucky for you, your father's butler, John, was there and killed the only man who had the cojones to try to stop all this!"

"Why the Mylanta is the Natas chip so important in the Master's plan?" I asked.

"Where is God's domain and where is the Master's domain, Victor?"

"Why do you ask me such a stupid question?" I asked, thoroughly annoyed.

"For you to imply that it's a stupid question is to imply that it has a simple answer, one that all should know—is that correct?" Dr. Juliard pressed further.

"Yes! God's domain is in heaven and the Master's is in hell!" I snorted.

"You are only half right, Victor. Yes, there is a heaven and a hell, but the true battleground is right here. God wants to give and receive love from his creation, man. All the Master wants is sheer numbers, mass over quality. He believes that sheer numbers will win the war of heaven and hell over earth. The Master hates all humans except for those who devote their lives to crushing God. The Natas chip in and of itself is not necessarily evil. It is more of a symbol that people will bow down to the ways of the world instead of to God. All Satan has to do is keep people's eyes off of God … and he wins! It's that simple. Sure, sometimes it seems more elaborate than that, but when you get down to the basics, it's really not. All Satan has to do is keep you occupied … and he has millions upon billions of ways and things—especially things—to keep your eyes off God.

"Think of a given person's day. For the sake of argument, we will pick a person who starts their day at six o'clock. They get out of bed, stumble down the stairs, and make themselves some coffee. They take a shower, get dressed, have breakfast, drive to work. They work all day, take a couple of breaks, check Facebook and their e-mail, and text friends with superficial, meaningless banter on company time. At four o'clock they drive home, and maybe they have dinner with their family. They clean up a little, watch television or a movie until about ten, and go upstairs to bed. Day after day after day, this is their life.

"Who did they talk to, or better yet, who did they have any influence on? Who had any influence on them? Where was God in all of this? Did they ever even look up? Did they ever take their eyes off the things of this world? That's all ... we have ... to do ...," Dr. Juliard said slowly. "That's all we have to do: keep their eyes on the things of this world, and they will be so preoccupied that they'll never even feel heaven slip through their fingers as they slip into hell.

"Let me ask you this, Victor: did you think it was a coincidence that the chip was called the Natas chip? Or that your grandfather and father went through six hundred and sixty-five other prototypes before they made the advancements they did in this one, with which the Master was finally well pleased? Open your eyes, Victor! The Natas chip is Satan's chip! With his number stamped on every chip! His number six hundred and sixty-six, stamped on the right hand or forehead of all who have the Natas chip implanted in them! The ink on the chip is a dye that will react and slowly seep through the skin and permanently brand or tattoo each person with the Master's number, six hundred and sixty-six! Only then will Satan's plan be exposed to the world, but by then it will be too late for them."

# Chapter 23

The second angel poured out his bowl on the sea, and it turned into blood like that of a dead person, and every living thing in the sea died.

The third angel poured out his bowl on the rivers and springs of water, and they became blood. Then I heard the angel in charge of the waters say:

"You are just in these judgments, O Holy One, you who are and who were; for they have shed the blood of your holy people and your prophets, and you have given them blood to drink as they deserve."

And I heard the altar respond: "Yes, Lord God Almighty, true and just are your judgments."

The fourth angel poured out his bowl on the sun, and the sun was allowed to scorch people with fire. They were seared by the intense heat and they cursed the name of God, who had control over these plagues, but they refused to repent and glorify him.

The fifth angel poured out his bowl on the throne of the beast, and its kingdom was plunged into darkness. People gnawed their tongues in agony and cursed the God of heaven because of their pains and their sores, but they refused to repent of what they had done. (Revelation 16:3–11)

God had been having a laugh lately, it seemed. First he turned the seas to blood, killing everything in them, and then the rivers and springs. The thing of it is, those who want to follow God will follow him, and those who don't, won't, even if it kills them. You could have all the evidence in the world that God exists, but they want to be their own god. After all, I've heard it said on many occasions that the whole earth and everything in it and on it is a testimony to the fact that God exists. All of creation cries out there is a God, but I said, "So what!"

We teach Darwin's theories and pick and choose from things he said and teach them in our schools. But what school did anyone go to that said that after Darwin studied the human eye, he said, "The complexity of the human eye alone is proof that there has to be a superior being?"

It means that all these complexities couldn't all happen just by chance. As much as I hate God, I still believed in him. Even Satan believes in God. At the thought of this, I laughed, but it didn't mean that Satan was ever going to make it back into heaven. I'd picked my side. You could have your so-called riches in heaven if he chose to let you in, but I planned to bank on my riches right here, thank you.

Besides, like I said, the majority of people here on earth chose not to believe or follow God anymore. I could tell them anything and they'd believe it as long as I didn't tell them that God did it. Once again I laughed.

So whenever anything bad happened, I just had to imply that China had something to do with it. But this one was gonna be a little harder to spin. How was I going to blame China for this?

I stepped out onto my terrace and closed the glass door behind me. Immediately, my bare feet started to blister from the intense heat. As I screamed in pain, I reached for the door, which had somehow locked behind me. *How is this possible?* I screamed as loud as I could for someone to help me. As the seconds passed by, I felt the extreme heat of the sun beating down on my bald head. I felt like I was in an oven on full blast, trapped with nowhere to go! The glass was bulletproof to prevent assassination attempts, but I picked up a metal chair to try to break it anyway. Again I screamed in pain. My hands seemed to melt as I grabbed the chair firmly to throw it at the glass. The chair didn't even make a scratch, and bounced off the glass. All I could do was scream. Every second that passed by, I felt my sanity slip away as all I could think about was the pain.

It was too high up for me to even conceive that I would live if I tried to jump, but as the seconds passed by, I didn't care anymore. I started running straight for the edge even though I could feel my feet sticking to the tiles with each step. I couldn't take it anymore; I would have to end it, even if that meant being splatted on the pavement ten floors below.

"Victor, stop! Stop, Victor! I'm coming!" I heard my chauffeur, John, call out behind me. I turned and looked over my left shoulder as I was running full tilt toward the wall that I would have to jump to achieve my death. I tried to slow down, but I stumbled, and my feet slipped with the melting skin. I slammed into the wall and knocked myself out.

John told me later that that was the only thing that saved me—knocking myself out, that is. Apparently the burns that I received would have sent anybody into shock and caused their heart to fail, which obviously would have led to death. I guess John is my guardian angel! Ha! I couldn't help but laugh out loud, even though it hurt so bad. My doctor said I had burns on more than 90 percent of my body and there just wasn't enough of my good skin left to graft over all the bad skin. I wasn't the only unlucky sap to step outside that day and burn his face off in the heat of the sun. But I was the only one so far who had managed to lose all the skin of his hands, feet, legs, chest, back, head, and face.

I was to be airlifted back to the United States to be operated on by a team of burn specialists. Dr. Juliard would meet me there. That evening while I was all drugged up on morphine, I took the long flight back to the United States from Israel. John never left my side and continued to watch over me. Around 2:00 a.m., I finally arrived at home via an ambulance that had picked us up from the airport, all under the cover of darkness and secrecy.

I asked John why we were at home instead of at the hospital, and he told me Dr. Juliard would explain. Just as Dr. Juliard had promised, he was there when I arrived. With the help of John, he helped me into the house and they laid me on the couch.

"I thought we were going to the hospital," I said.

"Like I said before, Victor, what God has done, no one can undo," Dr. Juliard said. "The best we can do is give you morphine and ask the Master to hide what God has done to you."

"Excuse my French!" I said. "This hurts worse than being crucified!"

"Really?" John butted in. "I can arrange that for you if you really think so!"

"Shut up, John! Know your place. You're just the family chauffeur! Or I'll have someone show you where it is!" I warned. "I don't care if you did save my life today, or thirty years ago! No one talks to me that way! Especially someone who works for me!"

"That's where you're wrong, Victor. You work for me!" I could see the rage growing in John's eyes. They started to enlarge, and the pupils were turning red. "You're not the only one who's been burned by God, you know!" His skin melted off part of his face and hands as he said, "*See!* When I had to save your sorry butt from frying on the terrace, I too got burned by God!"

"You know, John!" I shouted. "Thanks ... but no thanks for saving me! I'd rather have died!" I bellowed. I bit down on my tongue in anguish and felt the blood trickle off my tongue, mixing with the saliva in my mouth. That's the first time I tasted my own blood. With the intensity of the pain of my burns, I bit down again and it soothed my pains, if only momentarily. I bit again, harder ...

"You're not dying until I tell you you can die!" John yelled, and I swear he grew three feet in size as well as gained a hundred pounds. His body ripped and his skin tore open, and he appeared twenty years younger.

"Victor, you have no idea about pain until all of God's or all of my anger is unleashed on you!" His face started to change in a way I could only describe as a demon's as he shouted, "I am a living testament to the wrath that God can inflict!" That's when I saw that John was in fact the Devil himself. "Do you think I chose to look like this? Do you think I chose to be burned from head to toe thousands of years ago, only to still feel the pain today? Forget you and your pity party! You're not finished here until I say you're finished, so take your morphine and deal with it!"

I felt a sharp pain in my right arm and turned to see Dr. Juliard injecting morphine into my arm. After a few seconds, he helped me to my feet and walked me across the room in front of the wall mirror. He said, "This is how you really look," and at once I saw myself with no bandages and all burned up. "But this is how others will see you," he said, and at once I appeared healed although I still felt like I was in incredible pain. "You will only appear healed, for as I told you, what God has done, none can undo ... not even Satan."

As I turned to Satan, he was now John again, but his eyes shot Dr. Juliard a red glare that told him not to try to be funny or snide in his comments. The room suddenly turned to utter darkness as all the lights went out, and then the power went out throughout the city. All I could see was a slight red glare in the Devil's eyes as this too seemed to make him angry.

# Chapter 24

"The sixth angel poured out his bowl on the great river Euphrates, and its water was dried up to prepare the way for the kings from the East. Then I saw three impure spirits that looked like frogs; they came out of the mouth of the dragon, out of the mouth of the beast and out of the mouth of the false prophet. They are demonic spirits that perform signs, and they go out to the kings of the whole world, to gather them for the battle on the great day of God Almighty." (Revelation 16:12–13)

"Israel, what a curse you have been to me," I muttered out loud. It seemed that all I could manage was to mutter rather than talk. It had been three days of total darkness, and with the pain of my burns, my only way to cope had been biting on my tongue. There was no more morphine. My tongue was so swollen that I could barely talk.

John said, "The only way for us to finally be rid of God's people would be to kill everyone and let God sort them out."

"How do you propose we do that?" I said.

"The way has been made easy for us now that the great river Euphrates has dried up … We do it the same way it's been done before," he said. "War … All we have to do is whisper in the ears of Israel's enemies that we will finally give them Israel, and as a bonus, we'll let them kill every last one of them! Ha ha haaa!" Satan practically rolled on the floor in laughter and delight. "All you'll have to do is what American President's have ever done."

"What's that?" I asked.

"Lie … and supply the guns! HA ha ha ha," he laughed, and then he laughed again as one does when they find themselves funny and laugh at their own wit … "Just lay the groundwork," he said. "Make sure they're all ready when the time comes and Juliard … Juliard!"

"What?" Dr. Juliard asked.

"Make sure you do your part to a T," John said.

"What do you mean?"

"All you have to do is twist those Arabs' minds so they believe it's a holy war … The jihad … It shouldn't take much!" John laughed again. Satan sure thought he was funny …

> "'Look, I come like a thief! Blessed is the one who stays awake and remains clothed, so as not to go naked and be shamefully exposed.' Then they gathered the kings together to the place that in Hebrew is called Armageddon."
> (Revelation 16:15–16)

# Chapter 25

The seventh angel poured out his bowl into the air, and out of the temple came a loud voice from the throne, saying, "It is done!" Then there came flashes of lightning, rumblings, peals of thunder and a severe earthquake. No earthquake like it has ever occurred since mankind has been on earth, so tremendous was the quake. The great city split into three parts, and the cities of the nations collapsed. God remembered Babylon the Great and gave her the cup filled with the wine of the fury of his wrath. Every island fled away and the mountains could not be found. From the sky huge hailstones, each weighing about a hundred pounds (or about 45 kilograms) fell on people. And they cursed God on account of the plague of hail, because the plague was so terrible. (Revelation 16:14–18)

God's plans were different from Satan's, it seemed. While we spent our time plotting and scheming to raise up the world's armies against Israel on June 1, 2061, a great earthquake happened that left no one untouched. Never had a greater earthquake happened on the earth. Every great city collapsed, and not a building was left standing. Every bridge and every tunnel was destroyed. All the great monuments were destroyed, from the Pyramids to the Great Wall of China, including Mt. Rushmore and the Statue of Liberty. Every symbol of progress was destroyed. Every mountain crumbled upon itself, and even the islands disappeared into the sea. Hawaii and Japan were as lost as the great city of Atlantis. In Japan alone, 127 million people were killed by a tsunami that destroyed every living creature in its path. Hail the size of small boulders rained down all over the earth, killing thousands upon thousands of people besides the millions that the earthquake and tsunamis killed.

It was estimated that it would takes us more than eighty years to rebuild America to her former glory. It was decided that it would be easier and more cost-effective to bulldoze over entire cities and build new ones in different locations. If we chose to go the other way and tried to repair each city, the experts all agreed it would take decades longer and, in their best estimates, cost twenty times as much. Some people sought God out during these times as disaster seems to cause people to do, but just as many if not more cursed his name and vowed revenge on the God who would do this to them.

Babylon, the Prostitute on the Beast

One of the seven angels who had the seven bowls came and said to me, "Come, I will show you the punishment of the great prostitute, who sits by many waters. With her the kings of the earth committed adultery, and the inhabitants of the earth were intoxicated with the wine of her adulteries."

Then the angel carried me away in the Spirit into a wilderness. There I saw a woman sitting on a scarlet beast that was covered with blasphemous names and had seven heads and ten horns. The woman was dressed in purple and scarlet, and was glittering with gold, precious stones and pearls. She held a golden cup in her hand, filled with abominable things and the filth of her adulteries. The name written on her forehead was a mystery:

BABYLON THE GREAT
THE MOTHER OF PROSTITUTES AND OF THE ABOMINATIONS OF THE EARTH.

I saw that the woman was drunk with the blood of God's holy people, the blood of those who bore testimony to Jesus.

When I saw her, I was greatly astonished. Then the angel said to me: "Why are you astonished? I will explain to you the mystery of the woman and of the beast she rides, which has the seven heads and ten horns. The beast, which you saw, once was, now is not, and yet will come up out of the Abyss and go to its destruction. The inhabitants of the earth whose names have not been written in the book of life from the creation of the world will be astonished when they see the beast, because it once was, now is not, and yet will come.

"This calls for a mind with wisdom. The seven heads are seven hills on which the woman sits. They are also seven kings. Five have fallen, one is, the other has not yet come; but when he does come, he must remain for only a little while. The beast who once was, and now is not, is an eighth king. He belongs to the seven and is going to his destruction.

"The ten horns you saw are ten kings who have not yet received a kingdom, but who for one hour will receive authority as kings along with the beast. They have one purpose and will give their power and authority to the beast. They will wage war against the Lamb, but the Lamb will triumph over them because he is Lord of lords and King of kings—and with him will be his called, chosen and faithful followers."

Then the angel said to me, "The waters you saw, where the prostitute sits, are peoples, multitudes, nations and languages. The beast and the ten horns you saw will hate the prostitute. They will bring her to ruin and leave her naked; they will eat her flesh and burn her with fire. For God has put it into their hearts to accomplish his purpose by agreeing to hand over to the beast their royal authority, until God's words are fulfilled. The woman you saw is the great city that rules over the kings of the earth." (Revelation 17:1–18)

The other leaders of the C7 were very much preoccupied with the state of their own regions during the time that followed the great world earthquake, so they didn't resist much when I asked to step down from my position in the C7. I recommended Dr. Juliard as my replacement, and as they had all been quite impressed with him over the years, they were most agreeable that he would fit well within the group. With Dr. Juliard's help we persuaded them that I should stay on as an advisor and liaison between the C7 and the Arab nation that had grown astronomically in the last four decades and was now the largest religious group in the world.

Dr. Juliard and I had many meetings and talks with the ten leaders of the Arab nation, and finally on June 12, 2061, we signed a secret agreement with them. They would be allowed to destroy the Israelites once and for all, and we would not interfere in any way. Israel would once again be theirs. As always, in the American way, we would secretly supply them with any intelligence or weapons they needed in exchange for riches beyond our wildest dreams. Now was the time to act, considering the state of the whole world, but the only way it would work was if we took out the United States first.

The United States, just like all the other nations, was already on her knees, and all we had to do was cut off her head while she was down. For years I had poked and blamed China for everything. I insulted the Chinese by blaming all the world's misfortunes on them—the ones that were their fault and even more that weren't. With the help of my Society Brothers, we financed radical groups in China to create instability in their country. Many protests against the Chinese government were secretly funded by us, including a few assassination attempts. Some of it, ironically, was financed with China's own money. Every time I thought of it, it made me laugh. Who would ever know that for the past three years, I was secretly skimming tiny, unnoticeable, untraceable amounts of money from the Chinese people? Many years of orchestrating and moving the chess pieces just so would finally be revealed to the Chinese through an apparent computer program glitch. Little did they know that I had designed the glitch to be in the program; otherwise they would never come to the conclusions we wanted them to come to. My Arab friends played their part and exposed the truth to the Chinese about the assassination attempts as well as the role of the Society. Needless to say, I made sure I was out of the country by the time all this was revealed to them …

On June 14, 2061, China attacked the United States with every last nuclear bomb they had and destroyed any chance that it would rise out of the ashes. The Great Babylon had finally fallen …

Lament Over Fallen Babylon

After this I saw another angel coming down from heaven. He had great authority, and the earth was illuminated by his splendor. With a mighty voice he shouted: 'Fallen! Fallen is Babylon the Great!' She has become a dwelling for demons and a haunt for every impure spirit, a haunt for every unclean bird, a haunt for every unclean and detestable animal. For all the nations have drunk the maddening wine of her adulteries. The kings of the earth committed adultery with her, and the merchants of the earth grew rich from her excessive luxuries."

Warning to Escape Babylon's Judgment

"Then I heard another voice from heaven say: 'Come out of her, my people,' so that you will not share in her sins, so that you will not receive any of her plagues; for her sins are piled up to heaven, and God has remembered her crimes. Give back to her as she has given; pay her back double for what she has done. Pour her a double portion from her own cup. Give her as much torment and grief as the glory and luxury she gave herself. In her heart she boasts, 'I sit enthroned as queen. I am not a widow; I will never mourn.' Therefore in one day her plagues will overtake her: death, mourning and famine. She will be consumed by fire, for mighty is the Lord God who judges her."

Threefold Woe Over Babylon's Fall

"When the kings of the earth who committed adultery with her and shared her luxury see the smoke of her burning, they will weep and mourn over her. Terrified at her torment, they will stand far off and cry: 'Woe! Woe to you, great city, you mighty city of Babylon! In one hour your doom has come!' The merchants of the earth will weep and mourn over her because no one buys their cargoes anymore—cargoes of gold, silver, precious stones and pearls; fine linen, purple, silk and scarlet cloth; every sort of citron wood, and articles of every kind made of ivory, costly wood, bronze, iron and marble; cargoes of cinnamon and spice, of incense, myrrh and frankincense, of wine and olive oil, of fine flour and wheat; cattle and sheep; horses and carriages; and human beings sold as slaves. They will say, 'The fruit you longed for is gone from you. All your luxury and splendor have vanished, never to be recovered.' The merchants who sold these things and gained their wealth from her will stand far off, terrified at her torment. They will weep and mourn and cry out: 'Woe! Woe to you, great city, dressed in fine linen, purple and scarlet, and glittering with gold, precious stones and pearls! In one hour such great wealth has been brought to ruin!' Every sea captain, and all who travel by ship, the sailors, and all who earn their living from the sea, will stand far off. When they see the smoke of her burning, they will exclaim, 'Was there ever a city like this great city?' They will throw dust on their heads, and with weeping and mourning cry out: 'Woe! Woe to you, great city, where all who had ships on the sea became rich through her wealth! In one hour she has been brought to ruin!' Rejoice over her, you heavens! Rejoice, you people of God! Rejoice, apostles and prophets! For God has judged her with the judgment she imposed on you."

The Finality of Babylon's Doom

Then a mighty angel picked up a boulder the size of a large millstone and threw it into the sea, and said: "With such violence the great city of Babylon will be thrown down, never to be found again. The music of harpists and musicians, pipers and trumpeters, will never be heard in you again. No worker of any trade will ever be found in you again. The sound of a millstone will never be heard in you again. The light of a lamp will never shine in you again. The voice of bridegroom and bride will never be heard in you again. Your merchants were the world's important people. By your magic spell all the nations were led astray. In her was found the blood of prophets and of God's holy people, of all who have been slaughtered on the earth." (Revelation 18:1–24)

# Chapter 26

Threefold Hallelujah Over Babylon's Fall

After this I heard what sounded like the roar of a great multitude in heaven shouting: "Hallelujah! Salvation and glory and power belong to our God, for true and just are his judgments. He has condemned the great prostitute who corrupted the earth by her adulteries. He has avenged on her the blood of his servants." And again they shouted: "Hallelujah! The smoke from her goes up for ever and ever."

The twenty-four elders and the four living creatures fell down and worshiped God, who was seated on the throne. And they cried: "Amen, Hallelujah!" Then a voice came from the throne, saying: "Praise our God, all you his servants, you who fear him, both great and small!"

Then I heard what sounded like a great multitude, like the roar of rushing waters and like loud peals of thunder, shouting: "Hallelujah! For our Lord God Almighty reigns. Let us rejoice and be glad and give him glory! For the wedding of the Lamb has come, and his bride has made herself ready. Fine linen, bright and clean, was given her to wear."

Then the angel said to me, "Write this: Blessed are those who are invited to the wedding supper of the Lamb!" And he added, "These are the true words of God." At this I fell at his feet to worship him. But he said to me, "Don't do that! I am a fellow servant with you and with your brothers and sisters who hold to the testimony of Jesus.

Worship God! For it is the Spirit of prophecy who bears testimony to Jesus." (Revelation 19:1–10)

"On the very day that America has fallen, so too shall Israel fall to you, the kings of the Arab nation, kings of the earth!" I shouted. A multitude of millions of Arabs cheered and clanged whatever weapons they had brought with them for the annihilation of the Israelites.

Dr. Juliard was with me for this monumental moment to witness God's people's final defeat and he shouted, "Let us march across the Great Euphrates and conquer Israel and her God once and for all!"

Again the Arabs cheered. The ten kings of the Arab nation all shouted, "ATTACK!"

The Heavenly Warrior Defeats the Beast

I saw heaven standing open and there before me was a white horse, whose rider is called Faithful and True. With justice he judges and wages war. His eyes are like blazing fire, and on his head are many crowns. He has a name written on him that no one knows but he himself. He is dressed in a robe dipped in blood, and his name is the Word of God. The armies of heaven were following him, riding on white horses and dressed in fine linen, white and clean. Coming out of his mouth is a sharp sword with which to strike down the nations. "He will rule them with an iron scepter." He treads the winepress of the fury of the wrath of God Almighty. On his robe and on his thigh he has this name written:

KING OF KINGS AND LORD OF LORDS.

And I saw an angel standing in the sun, who cried in a loud voice to all the birds flying in midair, "Come, gather together for the great supper of God, so that you may eat the flesh of kings, generals, and the mighty, of horses and their riders, and the flesh of all people, free and slave, great and small."

Then I saw the beast and the kings of the earth and their armies gathered together to wage war against the rider on the horse and his army. But the beast was captured, and with it the false prophet who had performed the signs on its behalf. With these signs he had deluded those who had received the mark of the beast and worshiped its image. The two of them were thrown alive into the fiery lake of burning sulfur. The rest were killed with the sword coming out of the mouth of the rider on the horse, and all the birds gorged themselves on their flesh. (Revelation 19:11–21)

The Thousand Years

And I saw an angel coming down out of heaven, having the key to the Abyss and holding in his hand a great chain. He seized the dragon, that ancient serpent, who is the Devil, or Satan, and bound him for a thousand years. He threw him into the Abyss, and locked and sealed it over him, to keep him from deceiving the nations anymore until the thousand years were ended. After that, he must be set free for a short time.

I saw thrones on which were seated those who had been given authority to judge. And I saw the souls of those who had been beheaded because of their testimony about Jesus and because of the word of God. They had not worshiped the beast or its image and had not received its mark on their foreheads or their hands. They came to life and reigned with Christ a thousand years. (The rest of the dead did not come to life until the thousand years were ended.) This is the first resurrection. Blessed and holy are those who share in the first resurrection. The second death has no power over them, but they will be priests of God and of Christ and will reign with him for a thousand years.

## The Judgment of Satan

When the thousand years are over, Satan will be released from his prison and will go out to deceive the nations in the four corners of the earth—Gog and Magog—and to gather them for battle. In number they are like the sand on the seashore. They marched across the breadth (expanse) of the earth and surrounded the camp of God's people, the city he loves. But fire came down from heaven and devoured them. And the Devil who deceived them was thrown into the lake of burning sulfur, where the beast and the false prophet had been thrown. They will be tormented day and night for ever and ever. (Revelation 20:1–10)

## The Judgment of the Dead

Then I saw a great white throne and him who was seated on it. The earth and the heavens fled from his presence, and there was no place for them. And I saw the dead, great and small, standing before the throne, and books were opened. Another book was opened, which is the book of life. The dead were judged according to what they had done as recorded in the books. The sea gave up the dead that were in it, and death and Hades gave up the dead that were in them, and each person was judged according to what they had done. Then death and Hades were thrown into the lake of fire. The lake of fire is the second death. Anyone whose name was not found written in the book of life was thrown into the lake of fire. (Revelation 20:11–14)

Lucas and I (Declan) were raised from the dead a second time, but this time to reign with Jesus for the thousand years along with all those who did not receive the mark of the beast but had been martyred. I asked Jesus, "How is it possible that people will still turn against you after a thousand years of being surrounded by your love and guidance, and why would God allow this?"

Jesus said, "Declan, let me tell you a story about a father's love."

"A father had two sons, one was a godly man who tried hard to always please his father. Everything the godly man did was to bring honor and glory to his father all the days of his life. The father loved his godly child and promised him a great inheritance, far beyond what his godly son could comprehend or understand. His other son was an evil man. Everything he did was for his own glory. He often tried to hurt his brother and others like him. His life was filled with greed, hatred, lust, vengeance, and even murder. Even though his evil son made his father very sad, his father still loved him and all the days of his evil sons life his father pleaded with him to come back to him so he could share the great inheritance with him and his brother. Even though the father's love never wavered neither had the evil sons heart changed from desiring evil things. Both children were offered the inheritance equally but only one of them saw the great reward for its true value. Some hearts will never turn back to God whether it be a year or one thousand years. The reason a person lives their life on this earth is so that they can choose their own path freely. When the day comes that they die and they meet their maker, they will already know the path they chose, heaven or hell."

Jesus went on to say, "Each person chooses what or who they want to worship, or in more simple words, what or who they want to be the center of their life. Many people choose themselves to be the center of their life, and others choose possessions or other people, while still others choose God. Follow me and I will lead you to the Father. For I tell you the truth, no one gets to the Father except through me."

"Oh by the way Declan, here's your journal back. I took it from Victor before I threw him into the lake of fire."

## Chapter 27

A New Heaven and a New Earth

Then I saw "a new heaven and a new earth," for the first heaven and the first earth had passed away, and there was no longer any sea. I saw the Holy City, the new Jerusalem, coming down out of heaven from God, prepared as a bride beautifully dressed for her husband. And I heard a loud voice from the throne saying, "Look! God's dwelling place is now among the people, and he will dwell with them. They will be his people, and God himself will be with them and be their God. 'He will wipe every tear from their eyes. There will be no more death' or mourning or crying or pain, for the old order of things has passed away."

He who was seated on the throne said, "I am making everything new!" Then he said, "Write this down, for these words are trustworthy and true."

He said to me: "It is done. I am the Alpha and the Omega, the Beginning and the End. To the thirsty I will give water without cost from the spring of the water of life. Those who are victorious will inherit all this, and I will be their God and they will be my children. But the cowardly, the unbelieving, the vile, the murderers, the sexually immoral, those who practice magic arts, the idolaters and all liars—they will be consigned to the fiery lake of burning sulfur. This is the second death."

## The New Jerusalem, the Bride of the Lamb

One of the seven angels who had the seven bowls full of the seven last plagues came and said to me, "Come, I will show you the bride, the wife of the Lamb." And he carried me away in the Spirit to a mountain great and high, and showed me the Holy City, Jerusalem, coming down out of heaven from God. It shone with the glory of God, and its brilliance was like that of a very precious jewel, like a jasper, clear as crystal. It had a great, high wall with twelve gates, and with twelve angels at the gates. On the gates were written the names of the twelve tribes of Israel. There were three gates on the east, three on the north, three on the south and three on the west. The wall of the city had twelve foundations, and on them were the names of the twelve apostles of the Lamb.

The angel who talked with me had a measuring rod of gold to measure the city, its gates and its walls. The city was laid out like a square, as long as it was wide. He measured the city with the rod and found it to be 12,000 stadia **** [1379.5 miles] in length, and as wide and high as it is long. (Revelation 21:1–27)

The angel measured the wall using human measurement, and it was 144 cubits thick (216 feet thick). The wall was made of jasper, and the city of pure gold, as pure as glass. The foundations of the city walls were decorated with every kind of precious stone. The first foundation was jasper, the second sapphire, the third agate, the fourth emerald, the fifth onyx, the sixth ruby, the seventh chrysolite, the eighth beryl, the ninth topaz, the tenth turquoise, the eleventh jacinth, and the twelfth amethyst. The twelve gates were twelve pearls, each gate made of a single pearl. The great street of the city was of gold, as pure as transparent glass.

I did not see a temple in the city, because the Lord God Almighty and the Lamb are its temple. The city does not need the sun or the moon to shine on it, for the glory of God gives it light, and the Lamb is its lamp. The nations will walk by its light, and the kings of the earth will bring their splendor into it. On no day will its gates ever be shut, for there will be no night there. The glory and honor of the nations will be brought into it. Nothing impure will ever enter it, nor will anyone who does what is shameful or deceitful, but only those whose names are written in the Lamb's book of life.

## Eden Restored

Then the angel showed me the river of the water of life, as clear as crystal, flowing from the throne of God and of the Lamb down the middle of the great street of the city. On each side of the river stood the tree of life, bearing twelve crops of fruit, yielding its fruit every month. And the leaves of the tree are for the healing of the nations. No longer will there be any curse. The throne of God and of the Lamb will be in the city, and his servants will serve him. They will see his face, and his name will be on their foreheads. There will be no more night. They will not need the light of a lamp or the light of the sun, for the Lord God will give them light. And they will reign for ever and ever.

## John and the Angel

The angel said to me, "These words are trustworthy and true. The Lord, the God who inspires the prophets, sent his angel to show his servants the things that must soon take place.

"Look, I am coming soon! Blessed is the one who keeps the words of the prophecy written in this scroll."

I, John, am the one who heard and saw these things. And when I had heard and seen them, I fell down to worship at the feet of the angel who had been showing them to me. But he said to me, "Don't do that! I am a fellow servant with you and with your fellow prophets and with all who keep the words of this scroll. Worship God!"

Then he told me, "Do not seal up the words of the prophecy of this scroll, because the time is near. Let the one who does wrong continue to do wrong; let the vile person continue to be vile; let the one who does right continue to do right; and let the holy person continue to be holy."

Epilogue: Invitation and Warning

"Look, I am coming soon! My reward is with me, and I will give to each person according to what they have done. I am the Alpha and the Omega, the First and the Last, the Beginning and the End.

"Blessed are those who wash their robes, that they may have the right to the tree of life and may go through the gates into the city. Outside are the dogs, those who practice magic arts, the sexually immoral, the murderers, the idolaters and everyone who loves and practices falsehood.

"I, Jesus, have sent my angel to give you this testimony for the churches. I am the Root and the Offspring of David, and the bright Morning Star."

The Spirit and the bride say, "Come!" And let the one who hears say, "Come!" Let the one who is thirsty come; and let the one who wishes take the free gift of the water of life.

I warn everyone who hears the words of the prophecy of this scroll: If anyone adds anything to them, God will add to that person the plagues described in this scroll. And if anyone takes words away from this scroll of prophecy, God will take away from that person any share in the tree of life and in the Holy City, which are described in this scroll.

He who testifies to these things says, "Yes, I am coming soon."

Amen. Come, Lord Jesus.

The grace of the Lord Jesus be with God's people. (Revelation 22:1–20)

# Afterword

This afterword was originally the beginning of the story and was meant to provide a platform for an unbeliever to understand how Revelation could easily come to be. I also wanted it to end on the previous page so that God would have the last word, not me…

# Afterword 1

# Rise and Change

People started stealing gasoline more frequently when gas prices hit $1.25 per litre in the summer of 2008. They would simply fill up on gas and just drive away. Soon after that, there were cameras to watch every pump, and more and more often you had to pay before you pumped the gas. The price of bread, milk, and lots of other things went up too. All you had to say was that the price of gas to do the job or get the product to market went up, so everything else went up too. When I was sixteen, I can remember pumping gas for 49.9¢ a litre. In eighteen years, gasoline prices have gone up 265 percent.

In recent years the price of flour has doubled, and the price of fertilizers for crops has doubled and almost tripled in some cases. Where do you think we will be ten years from today? I really don't think it's unrealistic to think that the price of gasoline will hit $2.00 per litre by that time. It costs me $85.00 to fill my van and that's already steep. I can't imagine I'll be going anywhere when it's $160.00 a fill, and that's what some people already have to pay for their gas-guzzling trucks and sport utility vehicles. The price is always fluctuating, but if I know anything, it will only get higher.

The price of meat in countries has gone up as well. I read in the paper a while ago (August 28, 2008) that rat meat was up to $1.28 a kilogram. It's pretty bad that rat meat is even on the market, never mind that it's gone up 400 percent in Cambodia in the last year alone. Considering that Cambodia is a poor country and that the price of beef is four times more expensive than rat meat, it's kind of a no-brainer why it's on the market.

In July 2008, a friend of mine told me that a farmer was euthanizing thousands of pigs because it was going to cost him more money to feed the pigs than he would make when it was time to bring them to market. Another friend of mine who has about 4,000 pigs told me they lost $250,000 last year and $100,000 the year before. He isn't a dumb farmer, and he didn't overspend on machinery. If anything, he's about as streamlined as they come. Simply put, the price of feed to get each pig to market was about $50 more than what you'd get paid for a pig. You'd lose $50 per pig times 4,000 pigs = a minimum loss of $200,000 for that set of pigs that took you five to six months to get to market. No wonder people were killing them off. You would have to be well prepared for bad times if you expected to make it through. No wonder so many farmers fail after a bad year or two.

Through a government program, my friend has since closed down his pig operation. Even the government knows that the system isn't working, but they don't fix the market; they just remove the farmer from the market.

Biofuel has eaten up at least 20 percent of the US corn crop in an attempt to lower the dependency on fossil fuels. In Canada the conservative government announced up to $1.5 billion in incentives over the next seven years to get the use of ethanol up to an average of 5 percent of the content of gasoline. Sounds like it's really worth it to them if they're willing to dish out $1.5 billion, but there is a huge downside to using food for fuel. First off, that 20 percent of corn they're changing into ethanol is right now accounting for only 1 percent of the actual fuel.

I saw a related story on www.linktv.org broadcast by Global Pulse of a collage of news reports worldwide that said that it would take 90 kilograms (198 pounds) of corn converted to fuel to fill the average car—now get this ... *just once*. That same 90 kg of corn *could feed a small child for an entire year*. Thirdly the loss of that 20 percent of corn from the food supply is being attributed to the 10–20 percent rise in everything from eggs and milk to meat. In the end it seems that biofuels from food are definitely not the way to go, considering the increase in corn (up 31 percent), rice (up 74 percent), and wheat (up 130 percent).

Next they'll be telling us they want to try wheat as a biofuel. Food is for eating, not for shoving in your fuel tank, contrary to the Back to the Future movies where the professor is stuffing banana peels into his futuristic car. At least he was using the peel and not the banana …

What else is affecting the rise in prices? I'll give you 13.1 million reasons: that's how many people are being added to the global population every year at its current rate. Not a big deal if we were creating more farmland and generating more food, but we're not, and nobody else is either. That might explain why the global grain reserve has reached an all-time low of fifty-three days. All the grain that is stockpiled around the world would sustain the world's population for only about fifty-three days before there simply wouldn't be any more. That doesn't include the people we're currently already allowing to starve to death … Talk about mismanagement if I ever heard of it.

I guess the people in charge don't believe in being prepared for droughts, bad weather, or other things such as insects or pests. Maybe their mommies and daddies never read them the story of Joseph in the book of Genesis 41 telling of Pharaoh's dream. In the dream he saw seven cows sleek and fat, feeding on the grass, and then seven other cows gaunt and thin that came up out of the Nile onto the bank beside the seven sleek, fat cows and ate them up. Pharaoh woke and then fell back to sleep again. He had a second dream, similar to the first. In this dream he saw seven ears of corn on one stalk that were plump and good. After them sprouted seven ears that were thin and blighted by the east wind. The thin ears of corn swallowed up the good corn just as the seven thin cows swallowed up the seven fat cows.

No one in all the land of Egypt could interpret his dream except for Joseph (through God), who explained to Pharaoh his dream. The seven fat cows and the seven good ears of corn represented seven years of plenty in all the land of Egypt, and were followed by seven years of famine in all the land, represented by the seven thin cows and seven thin and blighted ears of corn. Joseph then advised Pharaoh to appoint an overseer to collect all the abundance of grain in the seven years of plenty to sustain Egypt through the seven years of famine. The amount that Joseph stockpiled in the cities was so great that it ceased to be counted. It sounds to me like it was a little more than fifty-three days' worth ...

China, what are we to do with you now? We've tried so hard to transform you to the ways of the West, and now you are. Instead of rice and beans, now it's steak and caviar. Everything of the West we have pushed onto places like China and said, "Try it, you'll like it," and then we can sell it to you. Trouble is, it worked. Now they want what we want, and it drives up the prices. Supply and demand: the demand is there, but the supply is quickly falling short and that will drive the prices up. It's not just the prices of our luxury food but possibly our luxury stuff, because when you want, you want more, especially when you're under the delusion that this stuff will make you happy. We've sold China on the idea that this stuff is what you need and it can make you happy, but we didn't sell it to one Chinese man, we sold it to more than a billion people. The population of China in January 2012 was recorded as 1,336,718,015. Source: geography.about.com. That's a whole lot of people to sell stuff to. That's a whole lot of mouths to feed something better than just rice, and a whole lot of wants to fill other than just a roof over their heads.

All this change is only the beginning. It seems like we've come so far technologically and strayed so far religiously. Sometimes I think today could be the beginning of the end of the world, according to John's Revelation in the Bible. Other times I think that it could get much worse before that ever happens. The truth is, it doesn't take long and it doesn't take much for dramatic change to sweep over the world. Think of all the things that could cause catastrophic change to our world.

Climate conditions such as global warming or, on the flip side, cooling can have devastating effects. A 10°C change in temperature either way and we'd have a major problem. Lots of the times here in Winnipeg the summer temperatures get up to 30°C, give or take a degree or two. During the winter, which most here would say is the other ten months of the year, temperatures can drop to -30 or -35°C. With the wind chill, which is when the wind whips that cold air around and seems to penetrate to the bone, they say it feels like -50°C sometimes. I heard that's where the lyrics from a Tragically Hip song come from: "Portage and Main, 50 below." Exposed skin can freeze in less than a minute in those temperatures. Imagine if it was hot or cold like that for months on end.

Now imagine if it got another 10° hotter or colder and stayed that way for a long time. The results have been and could be catastrophic loss of life when people are not prepared for temperatures of that magnitude. Most machines would break down or cease to even start at extreme temperatures. Considering how much we rely on something as simple as our house to be heated and cooled by technology, thousands or even more could die in a massive heat wave or extreme cold front.

War has and will continue to be a major player in the way the world is changed by it. There was World War I and World War II: what makes us so naive as to think there won't be a World War III? The only difference is that just about everybody has nuclear weapons and chemical warfare, which will result in the nastiest war ever seen in the shortest amount of time. More people could die from a war like this than all the other wars combined. Millions or even billions of people could die.

You really think that Osama bin Laden or any other terrorist cares that we as Canadians send our soldiers on so-called peacekeeping missions around the world? What better place to attack than a symbol of peace? After all, they attacked the World Trade Center, and what did that symbolize? It symbolized prosperity or maybe more important, the wealth of the West, so why not take it down? So, they did—with a lot of help, if you check out the top conspiracy theories. One of them is "Zeitgeist: The Federal Reserve's Five-Part Documentary," on YouTube. The whole world changed after 9/11, and that's the way they all wanted it to be. Just like most people who were around when JFK got shot by a lone assassin (another conspiracy theory), people know exactly where they were when the 9/11 attacks happened. The difference is that with 9/11 they burned it into our minds—9/11, 911, 9:11—so that you could never forget it. Every time the clock shows 9:11, I think of that day. It could be 3:11 a.m. or 12:11 p.m. I think about it. How many triggers do you have in your mind that make you remember September 11, 2001? Do you really think it's a coincidence? 9/11 changed many countries' policies on everything from passports to toothpaste. What will the next attack change? Believe me, it will happen, and it will change things. If Canada or for that matter the United States was wiped off the face of the earth by nuclear or chemical warfare, the fallout on neighboring countries would also be devastating. Millions of people would be dead, and millions more would die from the aftereffects. Nobody would come rushing to a country that's just been attacked by that kind of warfare. Self-preservation would kick in, and it would be too bad for you.

On a lighter note, I read an e-mail a while back that said, "Bin Laden: reigning hide and seek champion ten years, September 2001 to April 2, 2011." Bin Laden is said to have been killed in 2011. But if in thirty years someone says that for the past thirty years they had been torturing and extracting information from him, that would seem a lot more believable than the story the U.S. government told us. It doesn't mean it's not true, but considering their track record, I wouldn't put anything past them.

I heard it said this way: "A terrorist only has to be lucky once to have the opportunity to kill a bunch of people, whereas the government has to be lucky 100 percent of the time to not allow that to happen." The odds are totally in the terrorists' favor. My question is, Who made the terrorist in the first place? Bin Laden was a US-made terrorist, if you ask me. They used him to fight a war they wanted to win, and then they discarded him after they were finished using him. The only problem was, he had the means and the motive to exact his revenge.

Economically speaking, it is possible that in another ten to twenty years, China will be in a position to deliver an economic blow that would be felt around the world. China seems to have its hands in everything these days. When I look at product labels, they rarely ever say "Made in Canada." You maybe see it 1 percent of the time, if that. The rest of the world is probably not really much better either. China is heavy into computer chips and advanced technology. They also make an extreme amount of machinery, tools, and knickknacks of all sorts. They are slowly but methodically pushing many companies out of business with their unbelievably low prices—so much so that many companies have stopped making their own products. More and more you see "Made in China for So-and-So." The companies don't seem to be able to compete, so instead they just pass off stuff made in China as if it was their own, with the appropriate disclaimer, of course. Soon there will be no one other than China making those products, and after a while, they can start increasing their prices. Little by little the price could go up and up, because there won't be any competitor out there to keep the price in check. In many cases it would be too expensive to start a plant up again to make these types of products, so businesses and customers would be forced to pay the new inflated prices.

Dollarama is a good example of this, putting many small mom-and-pop dollar stores out of business and then finally raising their prices. Do you really think that any mom and pop would be stupid enough to open another small dollar store and think that they could possibly survive? Sure, there are a few stragglers who have not yet buckled to the competition of Dollarama, but think about how many have.

I bet you most people have never heard of a local Winnipeg company named Video Cellar, but a considerable number more would know of a video rental company named Blockbuster. Blockbuster had a store within a block or so of a Video Cellar store. Video Cellar lowered the prices of their movies, including new releases, to a dollar per rental. Blockbuster couldn't compete and went out of business. Another business opened up in the same Blockbuster location called Mammoth Video. Video Cellar kept their prices at a dollar per movie, and before Mammoth Video could even get off the ground, it was out of business too. This time Video Cellar bought all of its competitor's movies from them, and needless to say, nobody tried to open another video store anywhere near that location. It's a prime example of a well-executed plan. Video Cellar raised their prices back to their original, already-cheap prices, but just imagine if they had done it on a larger scale. There is no reason why they wouldn't become number one in the video rental industry. Update: The Blockbuster chain has since gone out of business. China has and could continue to flex their economic muscle and put a lot more businesses out of contention, and for that matter, out of business in the next short while. I've seen it in my own industry, and I've seen it in other industries, and I know it will continue to happen.

China also has another power, which is the power to control the market. At any moment they could stop selling vital computer chips and other such products. When I worked at Fountain Tire Retreading in Kamloops, British Columbia, we had machines with computer chips in them, not unlike a million other businesses around the world. When those computer chips failed, we always had to order the part from the United States. It often took three or four days to get the part, especially because it had to clear Customs on both sides of the border. That in turn shut our plant down for three or four days. Imagine if that part was never going to come because China wanted to inflict financial hardship or worse yet, wanted to put our plant out of business. Sure, they would lose out on the sale of the computer chip, but they could move in on our market and quickly take it over. That is just one example of all the possibilities open to them. It could put millions of people out of work around the world, and as long as China planned every angle and was prepared to weather the storm, they would surely come out on top. Drop a few nuclear bombs here and there after your enemy is down, and they'll have a hard time getting back up after that kind of a devastating blow. That would make it that much easier to walk in afterward and take what's left. If you fear no God, then what's left to fear? Nothing. This is not to imply that people in China don't fear God, it is only a hypothetical example.

# China Stockpiles Oil (Email I Received)

Scotiabank's commodities arm had forecasted $90 oil in 2010, based partly on China's intention to build stockpiles of the commodity during the next several years. (That number has increased to US$99 per barrel for 2014 said Patricia Mohr when I contacted her by email.)

"It has to do with organic growth for petroleum in China, but also other emerging markets like India and Brazil," Patricia Mohr, Scotiabank commodities expert and vice-president of economics, said in an interview.

"I do think that China will build stockpiles … it won't be a near term kind of gain. It's something that will be with us for a while."

China has completed construction of its Phase One tank farm, and appears to have five huge storage facilities along the coast, said Mohr.

China completed filling that farm by late last year, but a second phase of the storage is just starting construction. The massive nation will also build underground aquifers to store crude, and will start constructing those this year.

Next year they will begin the filling of those storage units, and then begin a third phase, said Mohr. (Patricia said in May 2014 "I have not seen much mention in the past year of oil stock building by China, but I assume that it has been ongoing.)

(I read recently that China has become more reluctant to share this kind of information, not wanting anyone to know how large its stockpiles are.)

China's consumption "…is now higher than the U.S. dependency," said Mohr. "The U.S. is going down."

The U.S. wants to move away from imported oil and has various policies in place to allow for that, including the production of corn-based ethanol, said Mohr.

"The real growth story for petroleum is going to be China, and then India, Brazil, Malaysia, Vietnam … the emerging markets."

(Mohr also said in May 2014 "that there has been a "sea change" in the U.S. oil supply picture in recent years, due to the advent of multi-fracture horizontal drilling technology -- which has allowed development of the

North Dakota Bakken and Eagle Ford in Texas and rejuvenation of the Permian Basin in Texas.")

Sources: The StarPhoenix. (email I received: Story dated June 30$^{th}$, 2009 Regina Leader-Post by Joanne Peterson). Also Patricia Mohr Scotiabank's commodities expert. (Email confirmation of original story May 2014).

## Hoax email I received:

I received an email about the Bakken Formation that had no author stated on the original email. After a short amount of research I found out through Greg at USGS that it was a hoax email that embellished and mislead about the facts. At the end of the email it did reference a real article that the USGS had posted on it's website. I cannot print the original misleading email here like I wanted to because of possible copyright issues etc,. I feel it would have been relevant to my story but with Greg's permission, here is the actual truthful information without any embellishments or misleading information.

### 3 to 4.3 Billion Barrels of Technically Recoverable Oil Assessed in North Dakota and Montana's Bakken Formation—25 Times More Than 1995 Estimate—Released: 4/10/2008 2:25:36 PM

Reston, VA - North Dakota and Montana have an estimated 3.0 to 4.3 billion barrels of undiscovered, technically recoverable oil in an area known as the Bakken Formation.

A U.S. Geological Survey assessment, released April 10, shows a 25-fold increase in the amount of oil that can be recovered compared to the agency's 1995 estimate of 151 million barrels of oil.

Technically recoverable oil resources are those producible using currently available technology and industry practices. USGS is the only provider of publicly available estimates of undiscovered technically recoverable oil and gas resources.

New geologic models applied to the Bakken Formation, advances in drilling and production technologies, and recent oil discoveries have resulted in these substantially larger technically recoverable oil volumes. About 105 million barrels of oil were produced from the Bakken Formation by the end of 2007.

The USGS Bakken study was undertaken as part of a nationwide project assessing domestic petroleum basins using standardized methodology and protocol as required by the Energy Policy and Conservation Act of 2000.

The Bakken Formation estimate is larger than all other current USGS oil assessments of the lower 48 states and is the largest "continuous" oil accumulation ever assessed by the USGS. A "continuous" oil accumulation means that the oil resource is dispersed throughout a geologic formation rather than existing as discrete, localized occurrences. The next largest "continuous" oil accumulation in the U.S. is in the Austin Chalk of Texas and Louisiana, with an undiscovered estimate of 1.0 billions of barrels of technically recoverable oil.

"It is clear that the Bakken formation contains a significant amount of oil - the question is how much of that oil is recoverable using today's technology?" said Senator Byron Dorgan, of North Dakota. "To get an answer to this important question, I requested that the U.S. Geological Survey complete this study, which will provide an up-to-date estimate on the amount of technically recoverable oil resources in the Bakken Shale formation."

The USGS estimate of 3.0 to 4.3 billion barrels of technically recoverable oil has a mean value of 3.65 billion barrels. Scientists conducted detailed studies in stratigraphy and structural geology and the modeling of petroleum geochemistry. They also combined their findings with historical exploration and production analyses to determine the undiscovered, technically recoverable oil estimates.

USGS worked with the North Dakota Geological Survey, a number of petroleum industry companies and independents, universities and other experts to develop a geological understanding of the Bakken Formation. These groups provided critical information and feedback on geological and engineering concepts important to building the geologic and production models used in the assessment.

Five continuous assessment units (AU) were identified and assessed in the Bakken Formation of North Dakota and Montana - the Elm Coulee-Billings Nose AU, the Central Basin-Poplar Dome AU, the Nesson-Little Knife Structural AU, the Eastern Expulsion Threshold AU, and the Northwest Expulsion Threshold AU.

At the time of the assessment, a limited number of wells have produced oil from three of the assessments units in Central Basin-Poplar Dome, Eastern Expulsion Threshold, and Northwest Expulsion Threshold. The Elm Coulee oil field in Montana, discovered in 2000, has produced about 65 million barrels of the 105 million barrels of oil recovered from the Bakken Formation.

Results of the assessment can be found at http://energy.usgs.gov.

This was Greg's original response to the hoax email I had recieved:

You've received one variant of the hoax/exaggeration messages that went viral several years ago. We were inundated with e-mails about this, and even wrote FAQs (http://www.usgs.gov/faq/taxonomy/term/9778) to provide accurate information. You do not need to obtain permission to use these FAQs, including the linked reports, (http://www.usgs.gov/faq/?q=categories/9778/3205) but please give credit for USGS material that you use. The e-mail itself was not produced by the USGS.

Snopes.com provides some background
(http://www.snopes.com/politics/gasoline/bakken.asp)history on how this hoax/exaggeration evolved.
Regards, Greg Durocher
USGS Office of Communications & Publishing
Science Information Services - Anchorage, Alaska

# Did you Know

Did you know: You Tube video with over 15 million views. 4.55 minutes Source: http://www.youtube.com/watch?v=cL9Wu2kWwSY&hd=1

China will soon be the number one English-speaking country in the world. The 25 percent of India's population with the highest IQs is greater than the total population of the United States, meaning that India has more honor students than America has students combined.

The top ten jobs in demand in 2010 did not exist in 2004.

We're currently preparing students for jobs that don't yet exist, using technologies that haven't been invented, in order to solve problems we don't even know are a problem yet.

The U.S. Department of Labor estimates that today's learner will have ten to fourteen jobs by the age of thirty-eight.

One in four workers has been with their current employer for less than a year. One in two have been there for less than five years.

One out of eight couples married in the U.S. last year met online.

If Myspace were a country, it would be the fifth largest in the world, between Indonesia and Brazil.

The number one country in broadband Internet penetration is Bermuda. Number nineteen is the United States. Number twenty-two is Japan.

We're living in exponential times (Definition: a to the power of two, one that champions, advocates, exemplifies).

There are 31 billion searches on Google every month. In 2006 this number was 2.7 billion.

B.G. = before Google

The first commercial text message was sent in December 1992. Today the number of text messages sent and received every day exceeds the total population of the planet, which is currently at 6.7 billion.

Years it took to reach the market audience of 50 million: radio thirty-eight years, TV thirteen years, Internet four years, iPod three years, Facebook two years.

The number of Internet devices in 1984 was 1,000. The number in 1992 was 1 million, and in 2008 it was 1 trillion.

There are 540,000 words in the English language, about five times the number in Shakespeare's time. It is estimated that a week's worth of the *New York Times* contains more information than a person was likely to come across in a lifetime in the eighteenth century (post of course in the *New York Times*).

It is estimated that four exabytes ($4.0 \times 10^{19}$) of unique information will be generated this year. That is more than in the last 5,000 years.

The amount of new technical information is doubling every two years. For students starting a four-year technical degree, this means that half of what they're learning in their first year of study will be outdated by their third year of study.

NTT Japan has successfully tested a fiber-optic cable that pushes 14 trillion bits per second down a single strand of fiber. That is 2660 CDs, or 210 million phone calls, every second. (Oh no—more telephone marketing!) It is currently tripling every six months and is expected to do so for the next twenty years.

By 2013 a supercomputer will be built that exceeds the computational capabilities of the human brain. Predictions are that by 2049, a $1,000 computer will exceed the computational capabilities of the entire human species.

During the 4.55 minutes of the Did You Know presentation, 67 babies were born in the United States, 274 in China, and 395 in India, and 694,000 songs were downloaded illegally.

Research and original design by Karl Fisch, Declan Mcleod, Jeff Brenman, gmvolt.com

# Sustain a Culture

Source: Muslims demographics: YouTube video with over 14,762,726 million hits. 7.31 minutes http://www.youtube.com/watch?v=6-3X5hIFXYU

The basis of this video shows that you need at least 2.11 children per couple to sustain a culture.

In France the rate is 1.8, England is 1.6, Greece is 1.3, Germany 1.3, Italy 1.2, Spain 1.1, 31 European countries = 1.38

Since 1990 in the European nations, 90 percent of the new population is attributed to Islamic immigration.

In France the rate given was 1.8, but the Muslim Islamic rate is 8.1 children. There are more mosques than churches, and 30 percent of the children twenty and younger are Islamic.

In 2027 one in five Frenchmen will be Muslim, and in thirty-nine years France will be an Islamic republic.

Britain in the last thirty years has gone from 82,000 Muslims to 2.5 million. There are more than 1,000 mosques and many used to be churches. They are up thirtyfold.

In the Netherlands, 50 percent of all newborns are Muslims. In fifteen years half of the population will be Muslim.

In Russia, 23 million people are Muslims, which equals one in five. Forty percent of the Russian army will be Islamic in a few years.

In Belgium, the Muslim population makes up 25 percent. Fifty percent of all newborns are Muslim. The government of Belgium said that one-third of all European children will be born to Muslim families by 2025.

The German government was the first to talk about it publicly, and released a statement. The German population decline can no longer be stopped, and it will become a Muslim state by 2050. Fifty-two million Muslims live in Europe, and the German government says that number will double in twenty years.

Canada's fertility rate is 1.6. Islam is the fastest-growing religion. Between 2001 and 2006, the increase of population was 1.6 million, and 1.2 million of that was immigration.

The U.S. fertility rate is 1.6. With the Latino immigration it is 2.11 or in other words the bare minimum. In 1970, there were 100,000 Muslims in the States. In 2008, there were 9 million.

Three years ago, twenty-four Islamic organizations held a meeting in Chicago. Transcripts there said we must prepare ourselves for the reality that in thirty years, there will be 50 million Muslims living in the United States.

The Catholic church has said that the Muslims have just surpassed their membership numbers.

Some studies show that in five to seven years, Islam will be the dominant religion of the world.

This video I also found to be uncorroborated and I want to thank the bbc.co.uk/moreorless for their story Muslim Demographics The Truth http://www.youtube.com/watch?v=mINChFxRXQs&hd=1 with 160,666 views which was in response to Muslims demographics: You Tube video with over 14,762,726 million hits. 7.31 minutes. Once again a video exposed for having half truths and uncorroborated information. If you will take notice, the original video has almost 92 times more views… As my wife said "You cannot un-ring a bell." Once a lie is out there, it is impossible to reel it back in.

The reason I have left these untruths in the story is because it is exactly that, a story. The other reason I left them in is because I believe we live in a world where we watch or read something and the majority of us immediately assume it's truthful. If we accept it as truthful then we register it as fact in our brain and never bother to corroborate the evidence.

# Afterword 2

# The World as I See It

Whoever said, "Don't sweat the small stuff" didn't know what they were talking about. Little by little the moral standards by which we were all judged and by which we judged others just disappeared.

When I went to school, you said the Lord's Prayer and we sang the national anthem, and if you really didn't like it, you waited out in the hall. Now they've taken God out of the schools and out of the courts. You can't even call a Christmas tree a Christmas tree anymore; if anything it's called a festive tree. But tell me how it is that our local school has adopted native Indian beliefs and is spreading the belief that the answers lie in the eagle's spirit and not in God. I am mocking the schools, of course, and not native beliefs; my own wife is native, and so are three of our kids. I often joke that I am a Heinz 57, and truly believe that most of us are a mixture of different nationalities. Many of us here in Canada are at least part native, even if your mom won't admit it!

More and more, everything is being politically corrected to death. You can't say this and you can't say that, you can't do this, and you can't do that because you might offend someone, so instead, we do nothing and we say nothing. For Pete's sake, every school is peanut-free because we all have to suffer to save the one kid who's going to eat Jimmy's peanut butter sandwich even though he's deathly allergic and his mother has warned him a million times. Teach your child not to eat peanut products; don't get the rest of the world to do your job for you so that you can sue them when your son dies from eating peanuts. Where are our priorities? It seems they're all tied up in the peanut epidemic. But let's let all the children starve around the world because we're all focused on Jimmy's peanut butter sandwich. Tell you what, let's send all the peanut butter to Africa and see if they send it back to us because a few people are allergic to it. Some people are deathly allergic to penicillin. Should we stop all the doctors and pharmacists from being able to prescribe penicillin? I know I'm taking it to the extreme, and I don't want anyone's kid to die from a peanut allergy, but come on ... Is this really at the top of our priority list?

Slowly but methodically, television stations have exposed children to all levels of violence and pornography in the ever popular if-you-don't-like-it, don't-watch-it mentality. They even make adult cartoons and show them during prime time for young children to be watching. The one I'm thinking of even has a high level of pornography in it. You can watch pornography on television any day of the week. Sure, some of it is illusively mild, but most leaves little or nothing to the imagination. Even a show or movie that I've watched with my family that seems like it's going to be safe for my kids to watch has gone from general to X-rated in 2.2 seconds. Does it really need to be there? I think not.

Graffiti is on every block of every street, unless of course you live in an upscale neighborhood. They'll spray-paint your fence, your garage, your car, or even your house; they simply do not care. It's gotten to the point that hardly anybody even removes it anymore because the taggers just keep coming back. It used to be that taggers tagged only trains, undersides of bridges, and stuff like that, but now more and more individuals are being targeted. If you think some things are still held sacred, you're wrong. Churches have been repeatedly targeted by vandals, and some have even been set on fire. Nothing is sacred anymore. I heard about a judge who let an offender off who had tagged multiple businesses in a neighborhood here in Winnipeg because he had a girlfriend and a child now and was sorry for what he had done. Nooo! He was sorry he got caught, and didn't want to go to jail. (October 14, 2010)

A while back now, a man was murdered on a Greyhound bus while on his way home from Edmonton, Alberta. The attacker stabbed him multiple times while the man slept. The bus driver did exactly what he was trained to do and got everyone else off the bus. Shortly after the police arrived and the attacker realized he was locked on the bus, he went to the back of the bus again. From there he went to the front and showed all who were watching his trophy: the victim's severed head. The attacker went so far as to eat part of his victim. Days later, while the funeral for the victim was being planned, members from a church in the United States came to the victim's hometown of Winnipeg and were planning to protest at the victim's funeral. They claimed that it was God's wrath coming down on this wicked man (the victim)! The protesters didn't end up showing at the funeral, but they had in the past, at soldiers' funerals in the States. What a sick-minded group, that they would seek to scar victims emotionally more deeply than any physical scar could go. The Devil uses sick-minded people to do his dirty work, not God. The Devil is hard at work, even in some churches, it seems. The killer was eventually deemed unfit to stand trial and admitted to a mental hospital where, I've heard, he has been an ideal patient. That being said, in my euphoric land it would've been a single bullet to the back of the head at his trial to save the taxpayers' money, or better yet a rage of bullets from the police officers once he showed his trophy to them on the bus.

Rape, brutal attacks, and murder are all everyday occurrences. The penalties for these crimes are so ridiculously low that they compare with petty crimes. You would probably get a longer sentence for tax evasion than you would for rape. I don't care who you are, man or woman, take a moment and just imagine what it would feel like to have someone force themselves upon you ... into you. How could you ever forget the violation! To me, most cases of rape are worse than murder. I can honestly say that I would rather be murdered than raped. The punishment should fit the crime, but it doesn't. I'm a firm believer that if you steal something out of want, rather than out of need, your punishment or your fine should be ten times that of what you stole.

Forced labor is fine by me. If you graffiti a house or church, you should have to pay for the whole building to be repainted, not just five bucks' worth of whatever color you can find that looks as bad as the graffiti that was just there. If you commit rape or other such twisted criminal things that make people want to throw up, you should be put down with a bullet to the back of the head—a shotgun shell, to be more exact. I'd rather pay two bucks on a shotgun shell than a million dollars to keep you in jail for the rest of your life. But it would probably not even be for life because some lawyer would get you off on a technicality. I've got a toonie for that schmuck too.

Willie Nelson sang it best: "For justice is the one thing you should always find. We'll round up all of them bad boys, and hang them high in the tree … for all the people to see." Justice has been lacking for a long time. The Day of Judgment is coming, although for some, it seems, not fast enough.

"Dear God, please forgive me for my sins. Please help me to prepared and not be lazy in your labor. May I be ready and not fooled by the false prophets, for when you come, the whole world will know, not only a select few who say, "Come, he is over here." None will be denied the beauty of your arrival, but many will be denied the rapture if they have not prepared themselves and are not already at the bus stop. What good does it do to start getting dressed and walk the walk to the bus stop if the one and only bus has come and gone before you ever even got out of bed! Lord, I pray that my brothers and sisters in Christ, and I as well, will be ready and waiting at the bus stop long before you come. May we wait patiently and not wander off. Amen."

# APPENDIX

The quote marked ** is from http://history1900s.about.com/od/worldwarii/a/hiroshima.htm. Two-thirds of Hiroshima was destroyed (by the nuclear attack in 1945). Within three miles of the explosion, 60,000 of the 90,000 buildings were demolished. Clay roof tiles had melted together. Shadows had imprinted on buildings and other hard surfaces. Metal and stone had melted. Hiroshima's population had been estimated at 350,000; approximately 70,000 died immediately from the explosion, and another 70,000 died from radiation within five years.

*** Denarius A penny or a denarius was the standard wage for a laborer in biblical times. In Winnipeg the minimum wage was $10 per hour in 2011. Ten dollars, times eight hours, equals $80 for a day's wages. Subtracting taxes, Canadian Pension Plan, and employment insurance would make it more like $54 or somewhere close to that. A measure of wheat was like two pints, which was sufficient for the daily needs of one person. In these days, a person making minimum wage will make enough per day to feed only themselves for that day. They won't have money to pay their rent, pay for gasoline for their car, or even afford a bus pass. It's safe to say that almost all low-income families will became homeless during this time and many people will starve to death.

**** Stadia. According to Dictionary.com, a stadia is an ancient Greek and Roman unit of length, the Athenian unit being equal to about 607 feet (185 m). A mile is 5,280 feet; therefore, a mile would equal 8.6985 stadia.) So 12,000 stadia divided by 8.6985 is 1379.5482 miles for the city's height, length, and width.

## OVERVIEW OF REVELATIONS:

- John writes to the seven churches telling them of their faults
- John in the spirit, goes into heaven and describes God, elders, creatures
- There he sees the scroll with seven seals, only one is worthy to open it (Jesus)
- First seal opened, rider on white horse bent on conquering and to conquer
- Second seal, rider on bright red horse takes peace from the earth (men slay one another)
- Third seal, rider on black horse destroys wheat and barley (sky rocketing food prices)
- Fourth seal, rider on pale horse (Death), Hades followed, ¼ of the world slaughtered by famine, pestilence, and wild beasts
- Fifth seal, the ones killed for witnessing about God cry out and are told to wait to be avenged
- Sixth seal, sun blackened, moon like blood, stars fall, every island and mountain moved, everyone hides knowing it's God
- Four angels hold back the wind, 12,000 from each tribe sealed (one taken, one left behind)
- Seventh seal, silence for ½ hour, lightning, thunder, loud noises, earthquake, seven angels given seven trumpets
- First trumpet, hail, fire, raining blood, 1/3 earth and 1/3 trees burned up, all green grass burned up
- Second trumpet, 1/3 sea turned to blood, 1/3 living creatures in the sea die, 1/3 ships destroyed
- Third trumpet, (Wormwood star), 1/3 rivers, streams, contaminated (bitter) many people die from the contamination

- Fourth trumpet, 1/3 sun, 1/3 moon, 1/3 stars destroyed, 1/3 of the day there is no light and 1/3 of the night
- Fifth trumpet, First Woe, star crashes to the middle of the earth, air darkened, locust torture only non believers for 5 months (death eludes people)
- Sixth trumpet, 1/3 of mankind killed by the troops (200 million) of Calvary, people killed by fire, smoke and sulfur, no one repents
- John told to judge/ measure churches, two men prophesy 1,260 days (3 ½ years), the beast makes war, kills the two witnesses (prophets), they are not buried, people celebrate for 3 ½ days and exchange gifts because they are dead, prophets rise up to heaven, that hour great earthquake, 1/10 of the city destroyed, 7000 people die, survivors terrified give glory to God (Secod Woe has passed)
- Seventh Trumpet, Third Woe, little scroll, John saw but told to eat the scroll so no one knows what the Third Woe is, ark of the covenant is in heaven, lightning, thunder, earthquake, heavy hail
- Great portent appeared in heaven (foreshadowing) Devil sent to earth
- Men worship the beast (Devil) rules for 42 months (3 ½ years)
- Mark of the beast 666, no one can buy or sell without the mark
- Jesus stands on Mount Zion with the 144,000
- Three angels tell the world to repent
- Many people put in the great winepress (wrath of God), seven angels with seven plagues (bowls)
- First bowl, painful, ugly sores on the people who have the mark
- Second bowl, sea turned to blood like a dead mans, everything in the sea dies
- Third bowl, all the rivers and springs turn to blood
- Fourth bowl, sun scorches (burns) men with fire, no one repents
- Fifth bowl, poured on the beasts kingdom, total darkness, curse God, no one repents, men gnaw tongues in anguish
- Sixth bowl, great river Eurphrates dries up, beast, false prophet, the ten new kings start gathering against God's people
- Seventh bowl, poured out on the great prostitute (Babylon), destroys the whole place that they will never rise again (every island fled away, every mountain could not be found) hundred pound hailstones fell on men

- Righteous and true on a white horse with God's army wages war against beast, false prophet and ten new kings, Jesus throws beast and false prophet alive into the lake of fire
- God's army slaughters the ten kings and every last man who stood against them, birds eat the dead
- Angel came down from heaven with the key to the Abyss and a great chain, binded the dragon (Satan) and threw him into the Abyss locking him in and sealing over it
- Jesus reigns for 1000 years on earth with no influence of Satan, the people who were beheaded for not worshipping the beast or receiving the mark reign with Jesus for the 1000 years
- Satan is released for only a little while after Jesus reigns for 1000 years, he decieves men and they gather with the Devil (their number was like the sand on the seashore) against God's people but fire from heaven comes down and consumes all the wicked men, the Devil is thrown into the lake of fire where the beast and false prophet are, they will be tormented day and night, forever and every
- All the books were opened, the book of life as well, the sea gave up it's dead, and death and Hades gave up the dead that were in them, each person was judged accordingly to what he had done, death and Hades were thrown into the lake of fire which is the second death, if anyone's name was not found in the book of life they were thrown into the lake of fire
- Then there is a new heaven and a new earth, a great and beautiful city better than we could ever imagine

CPSIA information can be obtained at www.ICGtesting.com
Printed in the USA
LVOW07s0505180216

475582LV00003B/76/P